THE BACHELOR FARMERS

THE BACHELOR FARMERS

Brenda Sorrels

Copyright © 2012, Brenda Sorrels

All rights reserved. No part of this book may be reproduced, stored, or transmitted by any means—whether auditory, graphic, mechanical, or electronic—without written permission of both publisher and author, except in the case of brief excerpts used in critical articles and reviews. Unauthorized reproduction of any part of this work is illegal and is punishable by law.

First Edition

Printed in the United States of America

Cover Photograph by Imantsu

Author Photograph by Vera Crosby

ISBN 978-1-105-42442-7

For Barry

Acknowledgments

I would like to give a special thanks to Margaret Doud for being my first and foremost guide and mentor. Her selfless, gentle, patient editing of manuscript after manuscript helped give this novel its life.

I would also like to thank my husband Barry Sorrels for his encouragement, love, and support, emotionally and literally—food, clothing, shelter—which allowed me to write and make this novel a reality. My stepdaughters are always there for me, and I am grateful to Quincy for reading all of my stories and being so honest and Avery for reading everything and helping to edit this book . . . and her honesty as well. Thank you to my sister Carla Friedman who has stood by my side through so many ups and downs in my life.

Ina Chadwick was the first real novelist I ever met and the first to publish my work, giving me the courage to pursue my own writing. She remains a huge inspiration. I am grateful to her for her friendship and support over countless years. Thank you, thank you!

Some exceptional, talented people took the time to read this manuscript with a critical eye and give me their feedback: Bari Ross, Cathy Vanden Eykel, and Angela Brady. Thank you all!

Evelyn and Jimmie Joynt, Sandy Lief, Beth Scott, Gary Udashen, Libby Miller, and the inimitable John and Carol Carr read several incarnations of my short stories, and I am grateful to them.

Lastly, we all have to be from somewhere, and I was fortunate to have been born and raised in the great state of North Dakota. This story was born out of the rich German and Scandinavian cultures there and in the neighboring state of Minnesota. It is a privilege to thank my parents, my large extended family, and all of the wonderful Midwestern people whose stories and zest for life inspired my writings and gave wings to my imagination.

The words that a father speaks to his children in the privacy of home are not heard by the world, but, as in whispering-galleries, they are clearly heard at the end and by posterity.

~ Jean Paul Richter

*** *Prologue* ***

Old man Gustafson laid on his bed facing a froze-up window, a blizzard raging beyond his gaze over the wintry black farmyard. An icy draft slipped in through a chink in the sill, sending a shiver through his frail body and causing him to turn slowly away. Scrunching the edge of the wool blanket, he touched it to a thin patch of grizzled beard then lunged his shoulders forward as if to lift himself, which he could not. He sucked in a heavy breath of resignation then dropped back as his eyes, clouded from days of fever, settled on the small group of sons, their wives, and children before him. Old man Gustafson was dying, and he knew it.

"My boys, where are my boys?" he whispered through parched, withered lips as one of his sons lifted the old man's head for a drink of lukewarm water that only dribbled down his chin. Another son rubbed the top of his father's hand as if to smooth out the dry, papery skin.

"We're here, Pa."

"Can you hear us, Pa?"

He gained a thimble of strength from the voices and hands that warmed him, but when the voices faded, so did his strength, and he shuddered in the bed he once shared with his wife, gone only weeks before. When he closed his eyes he was instantly lost in his own fog, clinging to a slab of drift ice. A weariness deeper than he'd ever known settled in his bones. He longed to let go completely, to slip deep into the watery abyss, but just as he was about to do so, a canoe wended its way toward him causing the choppy ice to shift and bob, rousing him back. A young woman, more Indian than white, with eyes as green as any sea, leaned down and with great strength hefted him up over the side of the canoe. Although she sheltered him quickly in a thick fur, heavy like the animal's body, it was the radiant light in the young woman's face that comforted him most. When she spoke, it was not the voice of a stranger, but that of his beloved, late wife. "Come, let me warm you," she whispered, and he felt sure that the sound of her voice was coming from her eyes. "There was never a doubt that I would find you."

The vision gave the old man strength, and when the fog of his dream lifted, he knew that in the shadows were his sons. The room felt full, bursting with this family he had created and loved, and his heart was aching with all that he wanted to say to them. Sorting through their faces, he searched desperately for the one final bit of parting wisdom he had the strength to share. Finally, he pushed the words out of a body long gone. "A father could not ask for better sons than you," he murmured, his voice rasping but managing to harbor a muster of the old grit he was known for. Sensing the urgency in what he was about to say, his sons leaned in closer, shifting the energy in the room so that not a word would be lost. In what felt like an eternity, the old man spoke again: "I have divided the land among you, so that you may not only live, but also thrive. Remember though, you can only *live* with the land. To thrive, you must love. Love is the most important thing, more important than the land." And having said his peace, the old man closed his eyes and passed over quietly at the first light of day.

PART ONE

MAHAL

CHAPTER ONE

There were four boys in the Gustafson family: Bjorn, Emil, Hans, and Jon. Their move to America in the final decade of the 1800s was motivated by abject poverty at home in Norway and the promise of the Homestead Act, which offered free farmland and ample fishing in the port of Duluth, Minnesota.

Hans and Jon, the youngest of the bunch, had not always been prosperous gentlemen farmers. Once, they'd been ratty boys born to nothing and left behind on the outskirts of Oslo with relatives no better off than they, while their parents and two older brothers squeezed onto a passenger ship with kindred settlers bent on new lives in the United States. The younger boys toiled for seven years, in and out of school, working fifteen-hour days bailing hay and mucking out stalls, Hans playing father to his younger brother, Jon, until their parents accumulated enough American dollars to secure their crossing of the Atlantic.

A week after receiving their fare, they booked voyage on the *Njord*—a rig that took a route similar to the one made by Leif Erikson himself—departing Bergen, Norway on a cold, foggy morning, then dropping anchor in Iceland, Greenland, and Newfoundland before landing in Boston Harbor three weeks later. There they caught a ride on a sturgeon sloop, only this time using their street smarts to hire on as deckhands, meandering the Great Lakes' Waterway to the shores of Lake Superior, choosing to slog and endure the stink of fish in order to pocket the fare of the passenger train.

The year was 1900 when they landed in Duluth with money in their pockets, and by the time Hans and Jon blew in with an abandoned boat dog in tow, in a vapor of wet fur, low tide, and beer, they found that the family members who had preceded them had already muscled their way into the immigrant population and laid claims on several patchy acres beyond the edge of town and the steep, rocky headlands that shored up the lake. The sheer joy of the arrival of the last of the Gustafson clan trumped the pain of years of separation, and the family hunkered down to the business of living— coming to know each other all over again, though Hans tended to be tight lipped and Jon a slip shy.

There was no time wasted in bringing the newcomers up to the level of the fold. Viewing language as the largest barrier to success in this new country, their Pa insisted that they only speak English in the house, and within months of their arrival Hans and Jon were thriving in the capable hands of their father and the overt love of their mother whose long-broken heart had mended the moment she'd laid eyes on her youngest boys.

"I can die in peace now," she told them more than once after their arrival, on nights when she would rest close to an evening fire studying their faces in the light, like an artist who had created a great painting. Through the years she had shed many tears. Her eyes still welled up at the mere mention of the word "Norway," unleashing an avalanche of memories of all the relatives and friends she had left behind in a world that she would never see again. The sweetness of her nature, though, hid an industrial will and an immigrant practicality that she shared with her husband whose lack of so much as a decent work horse back in the homeland fueled his vision of ownership in America.

"Ahhhh, my family." Their father puffed his chest as he eyed his sons many a dark morning, gathering them around the kitchen table where they slumped bleary eyed over their mother's brimming cups of coffee and open sandwiches. Often, he stepped around the table and lectured them like a teacher on the first day of school. "Boys, boys, there is a lot of work to be done, but at last, it is as I dreamed it would be. We are together in this new country. We own the house and the beds we sleep in as well as the land we live on." And then his great arms would open in a gesture of gratitude. "Here we can work hard and our hard work will pay us well. Here we can succeed."

As the years ticked away, firmly planted in this new country the boys matured into men, and the acres of Gustafson land grew exponentially. Bartering and badgering anyone and everyone for an acre of soil, the old man squirreled away cash and scooped up parcels and blocks of land, teaching his sons how to stake claims of their own and keeping a keen eye out for even the most unlikely of opportunities to expand. Before too long, the Gustafson patriarch was a sizable landowner—a destiny he'd only dreamt about back in Norway.

America had kept its promise of health and prosperity, or so it seemed, until the 1918 winter flu epidemic took both parents, one after the other, about as fast as bad weather could take a crop. By then, the Gustafson spread encompassed several hundred acres and included a compound with houses for Bjorn and Emil who had chosen wives of good Norwegian stock and had long since started families of their own.

Hans and Jon never had moved out of the family homestead. They bunked in the main house that now had numerous rooms to spare, and operated as their own entity, orbiting the rest of the family from afar. The familial threads ran deep, however, and the brothers interacted with a propriety of good manners, relying on family events and holiday gatherings to keep them all connected.

CHAPTER TWO

Bjorn, Emil, and Hans, the three eldest, collected in a dusty law office on Superior Street in downtown Duluth. It had only been a month since their mother's bad winter cold had taken a deadly turn, and within days, she lay fighting for her life. A flu strain, with a virulence no one had ever seen before, rushed cells and fluid to her lungs, rendering her family helpless, and suffocating her before they'd even had time to say a proper goodbye. Three weeks later, they waited and watched again as a high fever ravaged their father's body for days before he too slipped mercifully into a coma and passed away. The sudden deaths of their parents shook the brothers' resolve for a time, but life trampled on. And now there was a will to be read, and they were restless to get to it, waiting on Jon due in on the 3:40 out of St. Paul. Bjorn paced the room, pulling out over-sized law books from Ramsey Drake's overflowing shelves, then shoving them back, stirring up little squalls of dust as he went while Emil leaned sideways along the wall with his big hands dug deep inside his pockets, soundless but present with resignation. Hans had plunked down on a hard chair with his legs stretched out, arms crossed, eyes fixed on the Minnesota Territorial Seal that hung crooked on a bent nail next to what must have been Drake's law diploma, though the glass was cloudy and it was difficult to read.

"I hear the Northern Pacific drawin' up now." Drake cleared his throat as he pushed aside the window curtain with a carved duck-handled walking-stick he kept propped against the side of his desk. A patch of harsh winter light illuminated his pasty complexion, and he squinted for a view then checked his pocket watch, making a mental note of the time.

Without moving an inch of his potbellied body, he swiveled his chair for a clear sight of the tracks. "Looks like that city brother of yours might stay awhile with all those bags he's totin' You boys want a lick of fire-water, 'fore he shows up?'"

"Nah, we'll wait for the kid," said Hans who spoke of his younger brother as though he was much more than two years his junior. "Can't start the party without the family brains."

Ten minutes later Jon burst through the door trailing a rush of frigid air, stomping snow off his boots, and crash piling two oversized leather bags into a corner.

"To the land of milk and honey," Drake said as he laughed a big one and ran five shot glasses of Indian moonshine, inviting them to raise a toast.

"Skoal!" The men responded in unison, sharing a light-hearted moment before getting down to business.

"I've met many good men in my day, boys, but I never met a man with a clearer vision than your father. He had the integrity and determination to go along with it too." Drake raised a finger as if to caution them. "It's a cut and dried case we got here. He knew what he wanted and he knew how to split the land."

Drake shifted his over-vested body, and the wooden chair moaned as if at any second it might buckle to firewood.

"I'll just commence tellin' it like it is in my own way, and then you all can look over your own copy of the final decree of distribution at your leisure. You'll also get surveys and deeds of each of the tracts, so you can see what I'm talkin' about, where things begin and where things end, but here's what it is."

He leaned a solid right and threw back another swallow of the Indian spirits before rambling on.

"Bjorn, you'll be spreadin' west along the St. Louis River where I understand you already got a stake. There's a Titan's load of fertile farm land over there and some good bear huntin' I hear too. You can build yourself a brand-new, big ol' house and fill it up with those kids a' yours. Nothin' wrong with a life like that, 'specially if you got a woman that can cook, which I know you do."

"Now, Emil," Drake rearranged his mass and coughed dryly without bothering to cover his mouth. "You're to get the north end just short of Two Harbors. You got fishin' up there too. Should be able to do whatever you want: farm, trap, raise horses, cattle, kids. I hear you got another one on the way, so I guess congratulations is in order on that end too. It's all spelled out here in these papers, which I've carboned, and which I'm gonna' give you, like I said."

Drake's upper body hunched forward over his desk, his index finger moving down the page as it guided his eyes through the document.

"Hans and Jon, you're left the main farmhouse and the acreage just south of town, presently the 'Gustafson Corridor' as folks around here have coined it. Guess the old man thought he'd give you the roof over your heads, since you boys don't show much inclination toward marriage, like these here other two do."

"I must say though," he mumbled to himself, "with seventy-five hundred Norske's in this neck of the woods, you can't find wives?" Drake grinned, and coughed hard before continuing on.

"Your Pa didn't give up on you though. There is a provision here, should one of you ever decide to marry. You are to split the acreage down the middle and work it out between yourselves, which one will keep the house and which one will build on a new lot. The market value of the house at the time will be factored into the new one so things are kept fair. One thing's for sure, there's plenty for everybody."

Drake rested, peering over the documents, like a ship captain studying a map. A lone fly that had survived the winter freeze in some warm nook of his office sent a buzz into the room as it knocked against the glass under the cheap curtain, but Drake didn't seem to notice.

Bjorn was the first to speak up. "Well, our Pa sure did take care of us, and we thank you for your services, Ramsey," he said with an air of benevolence. Though Bjorn was the oldest, it was usually Hans who spoke first, but he stayed quiet this time and let Bjorn take the lead. Bjorn glanced at the faces of his brothers who nodded their heads in agreement as Drake cleared more phlegm from his throat and shuffled through the papers on his desk.

"Well, I guess that's about it for the land, and from here on out you're on your own," Drake droned on. "I've divvied up these bank notes too. Personal effects, what little there are, you can figure out for yourselves. You should all have everything you need to expand and set out on your own. There'll be some future signin' as I close out the estate, but I'll contact Bjorn when the time comes, and he can notify the rest of you," He lifted his eyes to make sure that Bjorn was paying attention and had heard him right. "It's been a hell of a year, and I speak my condolences, but you're wealthy landowners now, thanks to your Pa."

"Why don't you contact Hans for the signing," Bjorn suggested, turning again to the wall shelf and snapping shut the law book he still held in his hand, then shoving it back into the wall. "He's in the main house where the family records are filed, and Jon keeps it all sorted out when he's home. Just let Hans know when you need us, and we'll come on in to sign."

"Will do then," Drake nodded. He lulled a bit then rendered the desk a hearty stomp of his plump, raw hand. "My job's done, and I wish you all well. I'm the notary here too, so just sign on the lines and witness each other. Gimmee' your signatures and that's that for today."

Drake slid the final page of the will to the edge of his desk and dipped an old-fashioned quill pen into an inkwell he used for formal occasions. Leaning forward on his elbows he eyeballed them over the top of his spectacles, which had slid to the end of his damp nose. It was nearly ten below outside, but Drake still managed to sweat.

The brothers scrawled their signatures, then gathered up their copies and ambled toward the door.

"Oh sweet Jesus, I damn near forgot," Drake jerked back nearly toppling the squeaky chair. He rattled a key into the bottom drawer on his desk and pulled out a blue velvet drawstring bag.

"This here's the family crest. The only one it seems. Your Pa used all his money to buy land—was as frugal as a pilgrim in every other way, but he got hold 'a this here coat-of-arms. Hard to believe he bought it. More likely it came from some Viking relative down the line. Never did hang it, but I know he was proud."

He tossed the pouch to Bjorn, who turned it over in his hands with a touch of reverence before handing it off to Hans.

"It makes more sense to let Hans keep this over in the main house with the rest of the family business," he said to the group who voiced no objections and appeared to be comfortable with the arrangement.

Drake snuffed in a breath, noting Hans' steely cobalt eyes, the barrel chest, and hair the color of hay, long and tied back into a ponytail with a strip of rawhide. "Looks like an outlaw compared to the others," Drake thought, but he kept his judgment to himself and went on. "Well," he said, speaking slowly to Hans as if considering the possible implication of such a directive. "Usually the eldest son plays gatekeeper, but nothin's in writing 'bout that, so if you're in agreement that's fine with me."

When a "sure thing" from Hans satisfied him, Drake nodded a final okay to Hans and began the process of organizing the papers on his desk.

Hans cast a quick glance at the small cluster of brotherhood, then opened the pouch, revealing the colorful family plaque. In the short time since their Pa had crossed over, the brothers looked to Hans for leadership, and he had reassured them that things would be alright. Except for the long hair, Hans looked and acted more like their father than any of them, inheriting the old man's tenacity of will with an air of Viking toughness and drive. He knew how to delegate—how to get things done and had the physical presence to go with it. Large and muscled up, with a voice that carried deep, he didn't small talk and had a habit of playing with a small antler-handled knife that hung from his belt when churning around a situation in his mind. He wasn't shy on the answer either, which was almost always about right.

The brothers shook hands with Drake, thanked him again, then trooped down the tight staircase of the second floor office, pausing a block away on a street corner highlighted by the sun. Looking east down Superior Street, the blocks were lined with brick-front stores, hotels, pawnshops, and several saunas that catered to the Finnish miners, loggers, and railroad laborers who liked to unwind after a long day's work. Drifts of dirty white snow were piled up along the sides of the road, and in spite of the frigid temperature, people carried about their business undeterred, bundled up in scarves and woolen wraps knotted over heavy winter coats.

"I never imagined a day like this would come." Bjorn squinted his eyes in the bright light that reflected off the white tops of the higher snow banks. He shifted his body to break the glare. "But here it is. After all this family's been through." He paused to still the quiver in his voice. He would have been more comfortable expressing himself if he was alone with Emil, but that would not be possible today. Later he could go off and be alone with his feelings, even have a good cry somewhere in private. Emotional displays weren't something this varied band of brothers was comfortable with, and even this kind of talk was awkward. For a moment, Bjorn was back in Norway remembering the night Jon was born and the small square walls of his uncle's house and how they'd all sat scrunched together on the gathering room floor anticipating the wail of yet another newborn. Their uncle had taken them in when crops failed and their father had lost his job as foreman on a large neighboring farm. There had not been so much as an extra crust of bread at the supper table that night. Hunger pains had rumbled around Bjorn's belly, but he didn't care he was so thrilled to be there together at that moment. He almost grinned, picturing Hans—big and burly even at the age of two. It would be four more years before he'd board a ship for America, watching his younger brother as he waved from the dock.

"I dunno," he said as he snapped out of it, kicking a clump of snow to the curb as if to shake the memories from his brain. "I guess I thought they'd live forever."

"I think Pa, himself, thought he'd live forever," said Emil over the rattle of a trolley car jerking its way up the street. Somewhere off in the distance on the rough, massive lake, a tugboat brayed hollow and mule-like. "I never knew a more determined man, or a harder working one."

"Or a man who loved his family more," Jon added. He'd stayed on the quiet side up to this point, still dragging from the long, drawn-out train ride in from the city. "He did right by us, never losing sight of getting me and Hans over to this side of the ocean. Made us a whole family again."

Bjorn tilted his head and closed his eyes to soak up the light, letting a thought collect. "The only time I ever saw Pa break down was when we had to leave you and Hans back in Norway. It was easier to feed two mouths than four, and Emil and I were old enough to work. We all would've starved to death if we'd stayed, but leaving the both of you damn near killed him and broke Ma's spirit in two."

"Comin' here was their only hope," said Hans who was impatient to get on and move to a less sentimental topic. "He did the right thing."

"Swore he'd never be poor again," Bjorn added before stepping back to hide the emotion in his face and take his leave from the group. "Sorry guys. I don't mean to break this up, but I got broken pasture fence rigged up with cheap wire. Got to get to it 'fore the sun goes down. You here for long, Jon?"

"Help me out here, brother." Jon slid one of his leather bags from his shoulder and handed it off to Hans to keep it off the snow, then adjusted the weight of the other. "I'll be around about two weeks," he answered. "Hans and I got some business to discuss. You 'outta bring Jorunn and the kids by once you get that fence fixed. I'd love to see 'em."

"I'll tell her," Bjorn coughed a cold breath into his fist, returning his full attention to the group. "Maybe we can ride by tomorrow."

"Sounds good."

"I'll say goodbye now then too," said Emil who always went along with the group no matter what, the way he thought his mother would have wanted him to. As second born, he'd felt the most aligned with her—going out of his way to smooth things over whenever the need be. He moved next to Bjorn, eyeing a sign hung from a heavy string in the window across the street: **"HOT SAUNA FIFTY CENTS"**. "I've been toying with the notion of a nice, steamy sauna, but this took longer than I expected. We'll see you before too long." He'd had enough of the family business for one day too, and now at this late hour, he just wanted to get on home to his overly pregnant wife, Marga, due at any moment.

"Call us when there's news," said Jon.

"Will do."

CHAPTER THREE

The youngest Gustafsons were about as close and different as brothers could get. Hans was more of a country rough-rider, while Jon was the more educated, since early on he'd shown an inclination toward books, and, as such, the old man had sent him to college in the burgeoning twin-city area of Minneapolis-St. Paul. Jon was testing out the banking business there now, though he'd always kept an eye on the farmstead he had come to love and the family he'd longed for as a child. His mind thrived in the hustle of the city, but his heart could never leave his aging parents or the tall piney forests and the feverish northern lights that crowned the boundless, yawning land up north.

Hans and Jon set off to the main house in a wagon hitched to a couple of team horses, Jon's leather bags pitched behind him in the back with a sack of luxuries from the city: Ovaltine, Hershey's chocolate, instant coffee, imported Scotch whiskey and a Sears catalog. At the last minute, Jon reached around and dug the Dewar's out from the sack and twisted it open. They passed the bottle between them to shorten the ride. A bitter wind had kicked up off the lake, and short, powerful waves lapped at the shoreline as the wagon rocked back and forth like a slow moving train. When they were half a mile inland and well beyond the lake, Hans broke the awkward silence that had sat like a third passenger between them since they'd left the street corner in Duluth.

"I guess we got our work cut out for us," he stated in his matter-of-fact voice laced with an undertone that sounded like he was eager to get moving. "I know Pa had his eye set further east, but we already got acres up north we don't know what to do with."

"I got an idea, Hans," said Jon straightening up and struggling to tame a copy of the Minneapolis Tribune he'd pulled from his bag, snapping it in half against the wind. "I think I've got a way to pull us into the big leagues and make us a barrel load of money too." He warmed himself with a slow draw of the Scotch before going on. "If we cleared some of our forested parcels, we could expand. You know, clear more land, sell the timber, plant some of it up, use the rest as grazing acreage for more cattle, which, if done right, could turn into cash."

"It takes a lot of money up front to open land like that." Hans' jaw set tight as he reached his hand out and Jon pressed the bottle into his open palm. For all his bluster, Hans sounded more concerned about business than Jon had ever heard him, as if the reality of running things without their Pa was beginning to set in.

"I realize that," Jon plowed on, exhilarated by what he had discovered and anxious to share it with Hans. "But look here in the paper. You know the Ojibwa tribe . . . the Chippewa? Well, they're working with Finns, Norwegians, Swedes, and a few Frenchmen logging the white pines up around the reservation near Leech Lake. The logging company is looking to pay "stumpage rights" to harvest standing timber. I figure we can get that land cleared a heck of a lot faster and cheaper with their help. Hell, they'll pay us for the timber, and we'll get our land cleared." Jon wrestled the newspaper article into a square and waved it in the air to make his point.

"Let me see that," Hans reached for the paper as he pulled the horses to a halt and scanned the article with widening interest. "I'll be damned." He smiled a slow grin at this younger brother who, besides his brains, was more of a looker than the rest of them, with his wavy chestnut hair, classic profile, and a Norseman's strength of purpose. He possessed a benevolence beyond Hans' coarser ways, and presented with more polish, equally at ease in a suit or the shotgun chaps and boots he had hand-tooled years ago in St. Cloud.

"You know any big shots with the logging company? Seems to me we shouldn't waste any time on this one."

"I was trusting that's what you'd say." Jon relaxed his shoulders as Hans snapped the horses back into a walk. A patch of winter fog had misted in off the lake shrouding the afternoon light broken only by a red cardinal flitting in and out of the gray winter trees close by.

"Royson Lumber's the outfit I heard is looking to do business. The owner's a man named Arnold Royson. If you agree, I can give him a call and try to set up a meeting as soon as next week. Say, two o'clock at the Spaulding Hotel. I can even tell him to bring a contract in case we want to move forward, but I don't see any reason not to since developing the land's what we want to do."

"That sounds good to me. If it works out, little brother, we'll be in darn good shape."

"And Pa would be happy, too."

Jon's idea proved profitable, and soon they had a foot in the logging business, clearing and expanding faster than either of them had expected, with Hans overseeing the site work and Jon pushing the hard deals. This new venture was the excuse he'd been looking for to leave the banking to the suits in Minneapolis and return to Duluth. The move also left Jon time to indulge his love of books, for there was nothing that brought him more pleasure than a good read. His favorites by far were the books written by the American novelist James Oliver Curwood, whose fast moving tales of adventure captured Jon's imagination and spurred his love of the wilderness and the dangers therein. When he wasn't reading he was honing his archery skills along with Hans, taking after White Tail deer and elk in the hills near Spirit Mountain, keeping only what could be eaten and sharing it with neighbors as well as with Bjorn and Emil, whose growing families regarded the fresh wild meat as a delicacy.

CHAPTER FOUR

It had been almost a year since the early spring when the Gustafson boys had been able to properly bury their parents. Even then, the ground was still half-frozen, and it had taken six men to shovel-pick the loamy soil for their graves. By this time though, Jon and Hans had settled into a loose routine. In milder weather, most mornings, as the early sun rose up behind the farmhouse, Hans set out on horseback with his foreman who now lodged in Emil's old house. He spent the better part of the day surveying fields and fences, most often in the north quarter where calves tended to stray and many a timber wolf had picked a free meal. Oftentimes, he rounded up a couple of his hired hands and headed out for days, bedding in the logging camps, schmoozing the camp operators and tending to the business of being a landowner while Jon hung back at the house, scouring the newspapers for a good investment, overseeing supplies, keeping the books and payroll. To those that knew them, the brothers were looked upon as successful and eligible. Not many ladies came to Gustafson Corridor however, and the brothers never went searching, although if they'd ventured just five miles north to Duluth they'd have found a wealth of eligible young women looking to build a life with the likes of either one of them.

It snowed before Thanksgiving that year, which many took as a sign of a rough winter ahead. Early December brought more snowfall, half expected, but noted just the same, since the weather affected the livelihoods of so many there. It was three and a half weeks before Christmas, and Jon was up early scribbling a purchase list before splitting a pile of wood out back. The doleful granite sky and untamed winds left him fidgety. When the blade went dull, he honed it up for the better, but when the handle on the ax his father had used for over twenty years let go, he decided to head into town for a new one, maybe calm his spirit on the way. Then a better idea struck. Why not ride to the camp store, check on the logging site, and visit with their shopkeeper, Elias Mann, an old family friend and a Finlander who knew axes and knives as well as any man. Elias would sell him the best, of that he was sure. Hans had been to the camp regularly in the past few months, but Jon hadn't been up that way since the middle of August, and he was itching for a chance to see for himself what was happening at the site.

Whistling for his herding dog, Fjord, he decided at the last minute that he'd make better time without him, so he poured the dog a pan of water, penned a note for Hans, rolled a change of clothes and the leftover bacon and biscuits from breakfast into a kitchen towel, and by ten past eight, was shoving back the barn door. He slipped the bridle around the head of his quarter horse, threw a wolf robe over his coat to ward off the prairie blast, and set out, cantering in the blustering air, allowing his body to sink into the muscles of the powerful animal below him.

The sun had set by the time Jon walked his horse into the circular camp and strained the door of the camp store against the raw wind, sounding a bell latched to the heavy knotty pine. An old arthritic cat who lounged near the edge of a long counter blinked and lazily stretched when the door opened, and the uneven wood floor crunched under the weight of Jon's hard-riding boots as he lifted a glove to Elias, whom they'd had a hand in hiring as camp clerk. Elias Mann, bushy-headed with stains of Pearless running down his beard, was standing upright next to a woman behind the crude counter that ran against a log wall decorated with a rack of elk antlers. Elias was the kind of man you wanted overseeing a camp—one who could tell if a tree was rotten before the first stroke of an ax. Personable and good with figures, he'd been the only one to come to mind when the lumber company owner had asked the brothers for a recommendation. When Jon shed the wolf robe he'd used as an over-wrap and huddled up to the tall-piped stove in the center of the room to shiver the cold out of his bones, he noticed Elias low-talking the woman who appeared to be young and Indian. The girl faced him, but stood hunched forward, chin to chest, eyes set on the floor. From what Jon could see, she looked to be slight in build, but distinct, like a character in a clear and vivid dream.

"Hey, Jon," Elias raised up and motioned him over, eyeballing Jon straight on, taking in the faded buckskins and thick sheepskin coat, the most obvious sign of his prosperity. "What brings you up river?"

Elias liked the brothers from the first day he'd been hired on, appreciating their honesty and no-nonsense ways. They weren't nearly as stingy as their old man either, whom he'd known for over twenty years. Elias had been on more than a few Gustafson harvest crews, shocking up wheat in the scorching sun in the old days when his back was strong, and he could take the dirty heat of an open field. He preferred the forests, the cool shade of the trees, and the smell of wet bark. The big woods had been encoded in the genes of his Lapland ancestors, and his connection to nature ran so deep that sometimes the woods felt more like home to him than his own house. The years had taken their toll however, and now most of his days were spent in the rustic camp store doing his best to accommodate the loggers that drifted in season after season, some making it, others not, like prisoners on parole.

"Lookin' to see how things are goin' out here," Jon smiled as they grabbed hands across the counter, "and I need a new ax besides. Pa's old ax handle let go this morning. Guess it wasn't used to the feel of any swing other than his after all these years." His playful statement struck Elias, and they shared a friendly chuckle.

At the sound of their discourse, the girl lifted her face revealing eyes the color of sea glass that focused squarely on Jon for less than a minute before she dropped them to the floor again. The look caught Jon off guard. *What kind of Indian has eyes like these?* he wondered, feeling his heart drum inside his chest. There was power there as well as a vulnerability, and the combination confused and unnerved him.

"Got six axes off the Ojibwa reservation last week—Smokey Point up in White Earth. Made by hand. Let me show you what I got."

Elias hauled a medium size ax out from behind the pile of wool blankets on a shelf and laid it on the rough hewn counter. Jon watched him with distraction, for the Indian girl, who wore a printed dress similar to what the white women were wearing at the time, hadn't taken up her head again, and her dispirited air bothered him. She snuffled and brushed a strand of hair from her face with the back of her hand, then turned and slipped into the shadows of an open rear room.

"This here's the best," Elias went on, nudging the ax toward Jon, inviting him to handle it, oblivious to Jon's fixation on the girl.

"Steel blade runnin' clear into the wood shaft, keen as hell. You could fell a whole forest with this one alone and never need a honin'. I even got Canadians up near Lake of the Woods after these. Hell, I'll buy anything the Ojibwa bring in. No one makes an ax like an Indian. They know knives, and they know a good ax."

Jon nodded, keeping one eye out for the young woman. "Guess this is what I need, then. I'll take it," he said, slowly turning the ax over in his hands while huddling his back up to the heat of the stove. He dropped his head to roll the stiffness out of his shoulders.

"I'm thinkin' with the distance you've come you'll be spending the night," said Elias, who slid out from behind the counter and began feeding dry logs into the stove flame.

Elias was happy that Jon was there, hungry as he was for news of the world and gossip beyond the closed-in circle of the camp. "You can bed down with the log-men in the bunkhouse if you'd like. They'll be glad to see a boss, maybe hit you up for more wages." Elias chuckled again and rummaged behind the counter for an armful of skins. "I got buffalo robes should keep you plenty warm. Lots of provisions, too. The cook's served up salt pork'n beans and some high-raised biscuits and maybe I can scrounge up a nip or two later, just for us. Now, I know you like your Scotch, Jon, but cheap whiskey'll have to do."

Jon was fascinated by this new business of harvesting the wood, where burly men and more than a few fugitives spent the heartiest years of their lives housed in camps just to eke out a living—and happy to do it. He was looking forward to spending the night and experiencing the off-color camaraderie among the hireds.

"Sounds good, my friend," Jon responded, his eyes surveying the shady, ill-defined room where the girl had disappeared. "What's with the girl?"

"Huh?" Elias scratched his beard and turned to where she had been standing. He'd all but forgotten her in the excitement of showing off his wares to this important visitor who could appreciate a quality ax and would be willing to pay the higher price it would demand.

"Name's Mahal," he said, shaking his head in what seemed like irritation but was really only frustration. "She's a half-breed, married to an Ojibwa. Had a white father. I seen him come around from time to time years ago. A French trader from somewhere over near Big Sandy."

"Oh yeah. I know the place well."

"Crazier'n a loon. He showed me a picture of the Taj Mahal once. Carried it in his coat pocket and claimed it was the most beautiful thing he'd ever seen. Story goes he stayed around just long enough after Mahal was born to name her after the building. Can you imagine naming your daughter after a building? Not long after that he disappeared and never did come back. I dunno', mostly I see Indian in her, but sometimes I see white. In them eyes, I guess. Depends on what you wanna see. She's Indian more'n anything though, raised with the Ojibwa up north in Red Lake. Husband was injured three months ago in a timber move when a load of Norway pine cut loose off a sled piled sixteen feet high. Damn near died."

Hearing that the girl was married left Jon with a sinking feeling that only added to his unexpected overwhelming desire to know all he could about her. *She's so young*, he thought. The idea of her as someone's wife was the last thing he thought he would hear.

"Where was he injured?" he asked, raking his fingers through his hair to take out the dampness after his long ride.

"Right here," Elias cut a hand into the air.

"Our land, then," Jon responded.

"Well, yes. But ya know these things happen everywhere. Knocked the Indian silly. Injured his horse so bad they had to shoot him to take him 'outta his misery. It'll take the Indian months to heal. Don't know if he'll ever be as good as new. Word is he was already crazy in the head even before the accident though, either soft as a lamb or snortin' like a bull, nothin' in between. People around here talk about how he landed Mahal a black eye or two even before he got all broke up."

"Damn, Elias. That's not the kind of thing I like to hear happening on our land. Where's he now?" But Jon's mind was preoccupied with the picture of someone raising a hand to this quiet girl with the spellbinding eyes. There was something about her that drew him in—her long black hair, the way she moved like a shadow and seemed to look right through him at that first glance, the temper of sadness that hung in the air around her.

"Back on the reservation with his mother. Closer to you in Fond du Lac." Elias nodded toward the dim glow where the girl had vanished. "This one showed up here on horseback lookin' for work within days of the accident. As it turned out, it was perfect timing— my wife being laid up trying to hang on to the baby that kept threatening to make an early entrance. Martha lost a baby last year, and I didn't want her workin' so hard. Mahal's been here helpin' us in the store and some in the cook shack too all these months now. I let her sleep in the back room. Rides out to the reservation once a month and turns everything she makes over to her mother-in-law. She s a good worker and a good cook, but I can't keep her now that the baby's proving to be healthy and my wife's strong enough to come back to work. Thing is, I told her I had to let her go just before you came in. She's taking it harder than I thought she would. Seems as if she doesn't want to go home. As loyal as she is to her husband, if the stories about him are true it'd make sense she'd be in no hurry to get back to a life like that."

"So she can cook?" Jon asked the question.

"Hell, yes," Elias answered. "Speaks English bettern' me too, though I don't know too much about her other than what I've said."

"Hans and I sure could use some help around the house. We've been thinking about hiring a cook, too."

Jon surprised himself with his own statement, as the idea of hiring a cook had been the farthest thing from his mind. He and Hans had always gotten by okay, mostly living on stews and soups and an occasional cut of the prized venison from a deer felled on one of their hunts. Jon did most of the cooking, throwing together whatever they had on hand, but the sameness of it all was wearing on the palate, and the idea of a regular home-cooked meal was suddenly more than appealing. But even so, when there was a decision to be made, Jon was usually the cautious one, thinking it through, taking his time. He knew he should ride home and discuss this with Hans and then approach the girl, but he worried she'd be gone by then. And the thought of never seeing her again didn't sit well. Contrary to his better judgment, he knew he would do whatever he could to bring Mahal home, in spite of the fact that his hunch was Hans would not take to the idea of a stranger, a married half-Indian woman at that, living under their roof.

"That would be great," Elias jumped at the idea, anxious to clear his own guilt and make way for his wife to come back to work especially since she'd made it clear she hadn't been too thrilled about having this young, pretty woman working so close to her husband, half-breed or not.

"Mahal, come on out here," Elias called out as he moved to the center of the room and chucked another log into the sizzling stove, letting the metal door clang shut. "I got a gentleman here who wants to have a word with you."

Jon could almost feel Mahal hesitating in the back room, and for a moment he didn't think she'd come out at all. Slowly though, she stepped into the light. "What is it you want, Mr. Mann?" The question seemed to float from a voice so thin it was nearly a whisper.

"This here's Jon Gustafson," Elias told her, rubbing his hands together to rid them of the wood dust. "He and his brother own the land up here. They're good at business, but cookin's not their strong suit. No different than most bachelor farmers who care a lot about food but don't much care 'bout cookin'."

To Jon's relief, Mahal lifted her head. As dejected as she was, she couldn't have looked more beautiful to him, like a delicate child who had lost its mother and needed protecting. She held an air of wisdom though, the kind a person acquires when they have lived through more than their age would imply.

"I hear you've had some bad luck." Jon kept his eyes on her, eager to get some insight into how she felt about her situation. "I'm sorry to hear about your husband, but I think maybe I can help. Elias tells me you're a good cook, that you live here during the week and like to head back to the reservation when you can. An arrangement like that suits me just fine. My brother and I live near the reservation in Fond du Lac, and one thing we're missing is some good home cooking. We'd pay you well for your services. Does that sound like something you'd consider doing?"

"I am in a difficult situation, sir, now that there is no work for me here," she replied in the same small voice, again using the back of her hand to nudge the hair off of her face. "Do you mean keep your house and do the cooking?"

"Something like that. How 'bout just cooking and keeping the kitchen? That's all we really need. I can handle everything else. Heck, most of the rooms are empty now anyway."

"I have nowhere to work after here," she stated flatly.

"Well, that's what Elias tells me." She looked so forlorn, so serious, and Jon wondered what it would take to get her to smile. "You know," he laughed a little, "it sounds like this could work out well for all of us. We could really use the help. I'm surprised my brother isn't half dead by now, my cookin's so bad."

Mahal gave him a shy smile, just enough to soften Jon's heart even more. "When do you want me to begin?"

Within moments, she agreed to ride back with him the following day. The Fond du Lac Indian Reservation was about twenty miles west of Duluth and she would be able to return more easily to do her share in caring for her injured husband. Besides, she needed the money since her income had replaced her husband's these past few months and had allowed her family to purchase medicine and staples like salt, sugar, flour, butter, even clothing and sweets. They'd quickly become accustomed to these luxuries. Life for the Ojibwa had changed drastically after they'd been relegated to the reservations. With many of the old ways fading, the men had taken on work as trappers, traders, farmhands, and lumberjacks. And for their part, the women hired out as domestic help and did whatever they could to support themselves and their families, but money was always scarce and income unpredictable. The contribution Mahal made was gratefully received.

In the morning, Jon rose with the sun and spent the early hours after dawn riding the site with Elias who, invigorated by the cold, fresh air, jabbered non-stop in the open stretches of land where they cantered their horses. Half the time the wind swept away his words, and Jon missed completely what Elias was saying. But he was also preoccupied, playing different scenarios out in his mind as to how he would present hiring Mahal in a way as to convince his brother it was a good thing. He nodded and smiled though, as if he were attentive to Elias' monologue, his intention being to encourage Elias to keep talking and leave Jon mainly to his own thoughts.

"She don't talk much, Jon, but she'll do a good job for ya," Elias said as they came upon a part of the forest where loggers were already up and out working the white pines with two man saws. They pulled their horses to a stop under a swift layer of cloud cover that traveled across the sky high above their heads. Nearby, two hearty sawyers were pushing and pulling, working a fell saw on a tall, thick tree. The oily scent of kerosene mixed into the pine-scented air when one of the men called a time out and opened a flask on his belt to lubricate the sticky blade. "She has a way with horses, too," Elias rambled on, still referring to Mahal as they sat there watching the man. "Even the jumpy ones calm down when she takes 'em out. Damndest thing I ever saw. She rides better'n most men I know, too. Does a short ride every day. You might get her to open up if you bring up horses."

"I'll do that," Jon answered, suddenly paying attention to what Elias had to say, but still concerned with the bigger problem of how to handle Hans.

"Well, I know you'll appreciate the hot meals. You outta have her make some 'a that Indian fry bread, too. Martha even wrote down the recipe. Ain't nothin' better than that."

"I'm sure," Jon broke in. "But is there anything more I should know about her?" He shifted his weight in his saddle and turned toward Elias, running a deep pat down the side of his horse's neck. "There is something that's been bothering me."

"What's that, Jon?"

"You said her husband took his hand to her."

"That's what I was told," Elias answered, ratcheting his voice down a notch and meeting Jon's gaze eye-to-eye. "And she's come back with bruises on her a couple of times, but I don't ask. People's private lives are their own business, I figure. Whatever goes on though, it appears she still loves 'im since she's so set on heading out 'bout every chance she can get. I don't think she's missed once these past three months."

"Makes no sense that she could love someone that hit her," said Jon, shaking his head, hoping to convince himself that in spite of the fact that she was married there was no way she could love a man who had abused her. There were so many questions he wanted to ask Elias about her. Not wanting to appear too eager though, he focused his attention on the scene that was spread out before them and skill of the sawyers as they worked the trees.

They rested there, their own private thoughts disturbed only by the whistling sound of the saws in motion and an occasional shout-out of, "Timber!"

"There's a lot 'a things that don't make sense," Elias said. He turned his horse, indicating that he was ready to ride on, motioning for Jon to do the same. "Come on, let's head back to camp and you can have a bowl of her bacon'n beans before you hit the road and get a taste of her cookin' first hand."

The winter trail cut through a swath of birch trees whose bare branches allowed the morning light to dapple the snow with shadows that quivered and danced when the wind kicked up. Chickadees and sparrows chirped and hunted for shelter on the nearby pine branches as the men walked their horses through the snow. As he rode, Jon spotted a great gray owl camouflaged on a tamarack tree, and he took it as a good omen.

When Jon and Elias entered the cookshack, they were greeted by the smell of wood smoke and baked beans. Mahal was working with another assistant side-by-side the cook, an impatient man with a loud voice, though as Elias had pointed out to Jon, he'd never heard him mouth orders to Mahal.

"She's a better cook than he is, and her cookin' makes him look good," Elias had chuckled. "Come on, let's grab a couple 'a spots here on the end before the crowd runs in."

They sat down near the servers at one of the long communal tables that filled the room and was set with tin plates and cups. When the chef gave the thumbs up, his assistant blew the "Gabriel Horn", a long dented trumpet that summoned the men, and within minutes, a rush of "jacks" came barreling through the door, sliding one after another onto the benches that lined the tables. Working seventeen hour days, the men were allowed their fill, and as heaping platters were passed hand over hand, they got down to the business of eating the rich, heavy food that burned through their bodies almost as fast as they could shovel it into their mouths. The pace was frenetic, and the logged room was filled with the noise of clacking silverware and hungry men who preferred eating to conversation, raising their heads only to signal for another serving.

The highlight was a flavorful pot of bacon and beans that was attributed to Mahal, and it wasn't long before the men, including Jon and Elias, were calling out for more.

"It's delicious," Jon said to her when she passed him his second plate. "If this is what my brother and I can look forward to, we're mighty lucky men."

"Thank you," Mahal replied, smiling slightly as she started a basket of hot bread down the table. She kept a cautious eye on Jon, sizing him up and finding him to be a pleasant man, but still, men to her were as unpredictable as the seasons and so far there had been no exceptions.

"It's almost a sin to eat something this good," said Elias, heaping another spoonful onto his plate. "I wasn't lyin' when I told you she could cook!"

"You could win a blue ribbon at the county fair," Jon said, watching her serve the crowd as skillfully as he imagined she could ride a horse.

"It doesn't take much to make a hungry man happy," Mahal answered. But he could tell by the brightness in her eyes that she was pleased.

Chapter Five

After lunch and a short ride to view more of the cleared land, Elias and Jon trudged from the horse barn to the store where they found Mahal downcast, her long hair shadowing her face. She kept to herself, not speaking unless prodded, and even then, about the most Jon could get out of her was a nod "yes" or "no."

"Elias tells me you're a good rider, Mahal," said Jon, hoping to draw her out of her shell by referring to her "love of horses" that Elias had mentioned. He rubbed his hands by the stove in the middle of the room, speaking to her as she stood half hidden in the shadows of the back room with her belongings rolled thick into an Indian blanket and tied with a length of leather string. He was hoping to catch a glimpse of those blue-green eyes, but she never looked up. They were lost to him.

Mahal, sullen and wary of what lay before her, gazed on the dirty, splintered floor as if she were in a trance, her long dark hair trailing down her back like a cape, and a pair of deerskin leggings layered under her dress. The old cat leaped down from the counter, inching past her before disappearing into the dark room beyond.

"Elias said you take your pony into the hills nearly every day."

"You can't train a horse unless you ride him," she answered.

"So you like to work with horses then. Is that right?"

This time she nodded her head "yes," but still her eyes were downcast, and it was clear that this conversation was going nowhere.

Jon hesitated for a moment, unsure of how to break her near silence. He stepped away from the stove and faced her with his hands in his pockets. Somewhere in the far reaches of the log structure, beyond the mysterious back room, Elias' baby wailed for milk. "Is there anything special you need for our journey?" He asked.

She shook her head and finally whispered a quiet, "No, sir."

"Anything at all?"

Again, she shook her head, "no."

"Don't talk so much. You're making me nervous." Jon tried to elicit a laugh as he strode forward and hauled up her blanket role. "It's not like I'm taking you to prison or anything. Come on, Mahal, don't act so glum. Are you ready to go then?"

"Yes, sir," she nodded in agreement, and if his joking had made a difference, she didn't show it.

The silence that ensued filled the room, rendering an uncomfortable, stuffy feel. After several such minutes, Jon was grateful when Elias appeared, having brought up Jon's horse, fresh from a good night's rest, as well as Mahal's paint pony that she affectionately called "Wind." As Elias held the door, Jon and Mahal stepped out into the cold.

The temperature was well below zero and the pine tops swayed and bowed, bristling with sound and warnings of the angry gales that roared regularly across the haunting wide prairies this time of year. They rode within the protection of the big woods whenever they could, the pines and spruce with aspen and birch trees scattered in between, some reaching up thick and alone, others spaced close with their branches entwined like lovers in a dance.

"I like your style, Mahal," Jon told her after they'd galloped over a small hill, and he watched her ducking in and out of a patch of tall, thin birch trees to get to an open meadow. Wind was a quick horse, and it was clear he was anxious to please Mahal who balanced tall on his back, subtly shifting her weight to tell him what to do and show him that she understood his state of mind.

"Thank you sir. I have a good horse." Her reply was barely audible over the pounding of the horses' hooves on the frozen ground and the steady gusting wind, but Jon heard just enough to ignite a simmering of hope of more conversation to come.

After riding steady for a couple of hours, he was more than ready for a break. "Follow me," he shouted out to her, pointing toward a rough-hewn sign that had been painted with a black arrow and stuck in a snow bank at a fork in the road. They dismounted at Tannen's Camp alongside a half-frozen brook that still had a nice flow and rippled over large, round, blue and black speckled rocks. Tall evergreen trees that pointed to the sky were sprinkled throughout the campsite, but it had been cleared enough for weary travelers to take a break or in warmer weather maybe stage a picnic or even build a campfire and bed down for the night. They led their horses to drink at the edge of the stream, leaving prints on the blank canvas of snow. The trees shielded them from the wind here, and the sound of the moving water was calming, as if they had just stepped into a quiet room. When the horses were ready, they turned to leave, but as they did, Mahal slipped on a piece of ice hidden beneath the new fall that had been weakened by the clear running water. As her foot slid into the rocky slush, Jon caught her up and pulled her back to steady ground, overjoyed by this piece of bittersweet luck that had landed her in his arms.

"Oh!" Mahal cried, struggling to free herself from such a vulnerable position. She let the buffalo cloak Elias had placed across her shoulders fall to the ground.

Jon bent down and retrieved it, draping it over a large fallen log. "Let me see your foot." He motioned her to sit down next to him. "You can't ride with a wet moccasin. Your foot will freeze."

Mahal had three pair of socks on under her moccasins, which were less likely to freeze than rough leather boots. Being as they were now soaked through, she knew it was a different story. She sat down next to him and let him untie her moccasin and tug off her wet socks.

Her foot was small, and as he rubbed it to warm it up, he thought that he'd never felt skin so soft before.

"It's good now," said Mahal. "Thank you."

Jon reluctantly let go and covered her foot with the flap of his coat as he unwound a silk scarf from around his neck. The silk held the warmth of his body, and he was pleased that he had worn it, slipping it on at the last minute as an extra layer around his neck. "Silk is a great insulator," he said as he began wrapping it around her foot like a bandage. "This will warm you up." He then wound his way back to his horse and pulled a bowie knife and a curl of leather string from his saddlebag. Slicing a piece of the buffalo robe and layering it over Mahal's bandaged foot, he entwined it with the string. "This should get us home," he told her, satisfied with his handiwork. "It's not too thick. I think you will still be able to get your foot into the stirrup."

"Thank you." Mahal said again, lifting her eyes briefly in gratitude.

"Wait here a minute," he called to her over his shoulder. "Let me get us some water."

They passed a canteen of water between them and shared slices of dried apples that Elias's wife had packed and tied in a bandana. By now, Jon was growing accustomed to Mahal's silences, and he thought he could have been content to sit there all day with her. A gust of wind billowed up, as he indulged himself for a moment in this fantasy, sprinkling them with a flurry of snow and forcing them to ready themselves to move on. She straightened up then and placed her feet on the ground in front of her. Their shoulders were touching now and Jon was stirred by the modest connection. Flustered, he started back toward his horse as large flakes of snow began to fall lightly from the sky. The gales increased in intensity as they picked up their pace into Gustafson Corridor, the old homestead cresting into view just as the sun was veiling low over the dark, frosted hills.

CHAPTER SIX

The original Gustafson farmhouse was built on a four-foot foundation of river rock and stretched out like a cat on a flat piece of land five miles south of Duluth, well within riding distance to town off a dirt road that seemed to mud up at the first hint of rain. By the time snow fell, its many ruts made it downright treacherous with an automobile, so during much of the spring rainy season and for most of the winter months the brothers relied on a wagon-sled and horses to get them where they needed to go.

The house rambled in an inverted L-shape with the most used entrance on the far right. The door opened into the kitchen, which progressed left into a dining room with a large stone fireplace that served both rooms amply. Beyond that was what the family referred to as the formal parlor, although there was nothing really formal about this or any other room in the house. The Nordic-style wooden furniture made the house cozy but far from extravagant. Where the L took a turn, Hans slept in a room where their parents had once found contentment in each other's arms. Jon quartered on the main floor as well, down a short hallway where two smaller bedrooms were situated. An upper addition was built after Hans and Jon had arrived from Norway, featuring a carved balcony off one of the second story bedrooms that hung over the entrance door. A porch then extended below across the front of the house to the kitchen door. Inside, a tight set of stairs led down into the kitchen and another onto a landing near the true front door, though no one used it that way anymore, preferring the easy access of the kitchen.

The house was comfortable enough, and it was the only farmhouse in the area with an electricity line run out from the main line in Duluth. The brothers had financed it themselves. As carefully designed and well built as the house was, however, it was common during a heavy storm that the wind blew drifts of snow against the kitchen door trapping it on the porch. Coming and going was difficult. The entryway was clear now though, and Jon led Mahal in through the kitchen, where they were met by Fjord, who yipped and pranced at the sight of his master. The scruffy dog nearly knocked Mahal off her feet before high stepping into the water dish, spinning the metal bowl and splashing water across the linoleum floor like a wind-rush of rain.

"Down, Fjord!" Jon ordered his dog as Fjord marched and circled. "He won't hurt you, Mahal, he's . . ." but before he could say another word, Mahal was on her knees petting the exuberant dog's head, allowing his sticky tongue to catch her face for a kiss or two as she smiled and laughed—the dog managing to elicit what Jon had struggled so unsuccessfully to do. Jon laughed hard as he toweled up the floor, and for a second he imagined they might both break out into belly laughs. *You lucky dog*, he thought as watched Fjord pant in ecstasy as she scratched his ears and nuzzled his head.

"Would you like to see your room?" Jon asked her when Fjord had calmed down and he saw Mahal reaching for her blanket roll.

"Yes, sir," she replied, quickly returning to her more typical reserved demeanor.

She kept up, trailing Jon as best she could, for Fjord, who had perked up when he saw them take to the stairs, had appeared underfoot and was threatening to trip them up. At the top of the narrow stairwell, Jon showed Mahal into the front-facing balcony bedroom that had been whitewashed when Bjorn moved out. It was obvious that the room could use a woman's touch. As much as Jon had tried to convince himself otherwise, the moment he walked into the house, he felt certain that Hans would be furious over his bringing this stranger—this married woman—to live there. Now, more than anything, he wanted to settle her in before his older brother rolled through the door and confronted them.

The fading light of the low winter sun rayed in through the balcony door, and Mahal hung a dreamcatcher she had brought with her on the bedpost. The light shone on the purple beads sprinkled in the center of the web and on the dangling red feathers. Jon wondered what other treasures Mahal would bring into the house and marveled at how wonderful it already was to see this bit of color amongst the plain furnishings of the room. Ever since he had moved back into the old farmhouse, he'd come to view many of the rooms as dull and boring and had sent one or two more decorative pieces up from Minneapolis. Hans had been receptive to the over-sized club chairs in the parlor room, but after awhile his inclination to spruce up the place had been replaced by the time and energy it took to keep the business on track. Now, again he thought about how wonderful it would be to have a woman's touch reflected in the rooms. With so many considerations reeling around his brain, he almost felt out of breath. It had been a long time since he'd felt this kind of excited energy.

"Look, Mahal," he started in, for he was beginning to wonder if he would ever be able to have a conversation with her. "You're safe here. You can come and go as you please. We will pay you double what the camp paid. All you have to do is keep the kitchen and cook. Settle here and come downstairs when you're rested, and I'll show you around."

He was troubled now that he'd acted so impulsively. He imagined trying to explain the reason for his rashness to Hans. How could Jon argue his case when he hadn't much more than the beguilement of her eyes as his defense? But she was here, and she'd have to stay, he reasoned, at least through the night. His boots scuffed another layer off the worn wood as he maneuvered the narrow stairwell down into the kitchen to continue his worrying there.

Jon had no more than kicked off his boots, hung his wet socks, kindled a fire, and lit the wood stove, when Mahal appeared phantom-like at the bottom of the stairs. She had tied her hair up and wrapped a worn apron over her dress, presenting herself in the silence he had already come to expect. Mahal seemed almost dreamy as Jon walked her through the lower floor of the house, taking his time to point out the rooms, hoping, as always, to engage her. She only nodded politely though and waited for him to finish. Finally, when the tour ended they traipsed back into the kitchen, and Jon, acting on a hunch, dug a hunk of cheese out of the refrigerator and broke it up into chunks as he called Fjord.

"Up, Fjord," he said, glancing sideways at Mahal's face when the dog sprang forward. "Stay," he ordered, focusing on Fjord's eyes and balancing a square of cheese on the dog's nose. "Stay . . . stay." He repeated the words in a measured tone as he held up his hand and backed slowly to the opposite side of the room near the fireplace. When he was satisfied that his command was being obeyed, he looked at Mahal with a proud smile before moving on to finish the trick. "Release," he ordered and Fjord flipped the cheese off his nose, gulped it down, and sprinted across the floor. Mahal laughed a small laugh, grinned wide and Jon noted a spark in the gilded eyes that seemed to hold so much.

"You try," he said, passing a chunk into her hand. "Come, Fjord," he repeated and the dog sidled up to Mahal. "Sit, Fjord," Jon said. "Go ahead," he said, nodding to her. "Lay the cheese on his nose."

Mahal gingerly set the square of cheese on the bridge of Fjord's nose, and Jon motioned for her to back away and try the commands herself. At first her voice was so quiet it was surprising that Fjord even heard her, but, as if the dog too was anxious to make her feel welcome, he eagerly obeyed every whispered command.

Jon watched them play, stepping back toward the enameled wood stove whose flames were already adding warmth to the kitchen. As Fjord put on his show, Mahal's shyness began to thaw enough to make Jon feel encouraged that he had made the right decision in bringing her here.

Placing a hand on her shoulder to show her it was okay, Jon urged her on. "You may call him now," he said. "Go ahead."

"Release." Mahal clapped her hands together, and Fjord flipped the cheese and ran to them. "There, there. Good boy," she praised him, the light in her eyes brightening. They knelt together on the floor then, nuzzling the sturdy dog's head, complimenting him, showering him with attention.

This is more like it, Jon thought.

"You're amazing, Fjord," he said, pleased that his hunch had worked so well.

"Good dog," she repeated. "Good dog."

Mahal flashed her jewel-like eyes, and in that instant Jon heard his mother's voice: "If you want to know a person, look into their eyes," she would have told him. He could only think that Mahal was indeed an alluring soul, the kind that could make you forget the cold, the gloom, the harshness—the things in this land that people were willing to endure in order to have a place to call home.

"I will get dinner started now," she said, rising to her feet and running her hands down the front of her apron. Before long she had a small roast and rice bread in the oven alongside a winter squash, and while Mahal rummaged around the cabinets to find serving platters and bowls, Jon sat lingering at the kitchen table, inspecting a rare delivery of leather bound horticulture books he'd ordered from the city. He couldn't remember the last time he'd lazied around the kitchen like this. As the youngest, his mother had made him feel special by letting him do his reading there, shooing away the others, not wanting a pack of hungry half-grown boys cramping the small space and picking at her preparations before they were ready. She had always made a place for Jon.

He had just finished setting a marker on a chapter entitled "Fruit Orchards" when Hans steamed in, worn out and dirty from a day in the iced-over fields.

"Who's this?" Hans threw the question out right off, his hard eyes darting back and forth between Mahal and Jon, before settling on Jon as his mind worked to piece together a plausible explanation. His tone was earnest but not uncharitable, as he pulled off his thick, damp coat and latched it to a wall hook. Resting on the fireplace hearth next to his wet gloves, he leaned over to tug off his boots while waiting for an explanation.

"We have a real cook now," said Jon, pressing to sound nonchalant, pretending that coming home to a strange woman in the kitchen was no big deal, and that they'd been looking for a woman to cook for them for months. Knowing his brother as well as he did, however, he was certain that no matter what tone he used this would be a hard sell, even when Hans had heard the whole story. Still, it did not stop Jon from striving to figure a way to shed a good light on the situation. Before he could manage to do so though, Hans went right to the heart of the matter already suspecting that this strange woman with a full meal in the oven might be coming round on some kind of regular basis. "You live nearby?"

"No, she'll be living here for awhile," Jon took it upon himself to answer the question and spare Mahal a full-out interrogation. Careful to not act defensively, and consciously not letting on the real reason he couldn't leave this woman behind, Jon pushed on, praying that his tone proclaimed at least some measure of common sense and the conviction in his heart.

"Hans, meet Mahal," he said. "Her husband was injured on our land. She's been working for Elias since the accident, but he had to let her go." As a frown quickly furrowed Hans' brow, Jon hurried his explanation. "Now don't start getting too stirred up brother, 'til you hear the whole story."

"I'm sure there is one, but who says we need a cook? No offense to you ma'am," Hans threw a nod Mahal's way without losing a beat. "Your cookin' suits me fine, Jon."

He shook a worn out sock at Fjord who'd come sniffing around his boots. "Outta here, boy," he scolded, but his gaze was set on Mahal.

Mahal was crushed, inching back behind the square oak table, her mouth set tight, her eyes downcast. She'd heard talk like this before and most of the time it did not end in her favor. She knew the brothers would talk later, out of earshot to her, and when they did, anything could happen. Most likely, she assumed, she'd be on her way in a day or two, heading back to Fond du Lac, back to the reservation and the broke-up husband that languished there with no way to support him or his aging mother.

Hans scrubbed his hands in the kitchen sink, lathering up his forearms and splashing his face with the cold water, splattering the wall and worn down linoleum floor. He snatched a kitchen towel off a hook and rubbed himself hard as if that would somehow wipe away the long, cold day and the problem that had greeted him at the door.

The tension in the air was palpable and Jon was edgy, not as prepared as he hoped he would be to take on the forceful nature of Hans' personality.

"Let me help you serve up the food," Jon said to Mahal as she turned from the men and began tugging pans out of the oven. The fragrant scent of roasted meat overpowered the room that felt suddenly cramped and confining. To shield her from another round of questions, Jon grabbed a plate of bread warming on the cook top and moved into the dining room with Hans close behind. Hans dropped onto one of the hard wooden chairs, pushed it back with his eyes turned upward, uncharacteristically silent, the laser focus of his thoughts glaringly obvious. When the food had been set and Jon had taken his place, Hans broke his silence with a deep sigh and hauled himself up to the table. With deliberation, he hacked up his roast venison, stabbing at the potatoes while Jon chewed slowly as he tried desperately to convince himself that Hans was just being unreasonable. But the silence took its toll, and Jon hurried through his dinner, then quickly picked up his plate and returned to the kitchen leaving Hans to finish alone.

"Hans is still eating, Mahal. It . . . was delicious." Jon smiled. He set his plate beside the sink and gave it all that he had to put her at ease and assuage his guilt of bringing her into this situation. "You've done enough. I'll clean up these dishes. Why don't you go upstairs and rest. It's been a long day, and I'm sure you're tired. We'll talk again in the morning."

When Mahal had taken her leave, Jon splashed a couple of glasses of Scotch and rejoined Hans in the dining room where his older brother had pushed aside his plate and planted his elbows on the table, his big hands rubbing the sides of his forehead.

Sliding one of the glasses towards Hans with more force than he intended, Jon blurted out the rehearsed explanation. "Her husband's been injured on our land up near the lake," he repeated, the weight of his statement resonating in the room. "She needs work at least until he can heal. I learned of her situation yesterday up at the camp. Elias had hired her on, but he had to let her go since his wife's given birth and is ready to return to work. Besides, if you think about it, it's the least we can do."

Hans waited to let the words sink in. "How long do you plan on her being here?" he asked, impatience and frustration with the situation coloring his every word.

"She'll be leavin' when he's healed up, I expect," Jon answered. He felt angry at Hans' insensitivity, his failure to feel some kind of responsibility toward her—the fact that the accident had occurred on their land. "She plans to ride home most weekends. Husband's on the reservation at Fond du Lac where he's being cared for by his mother. It's a temporary thing. Just 'til he heals."

"Husband? She's married?" Hans replied, his volume increasing as he pushed his chair away from the table and stared hard at his brother. "People will talk, Jon! What were you thinking?"

"I don't give a damn what other people say. It's none of their business what we do, or who we hire."

"Well, a man's reputation is something to take seriously, and it doesn't look good for a married woman, an Ojibwa woman, to be living with two bachelors. White men at that. If she worked days and left nights that would be one thing, but living here . . . now that's something else altogether."

"But it's impossible for her to leave come night time. Forty miles round trip to Fond du Lac is too far to travel every day. That won't work. She'll head up there on the weekends, but not during the week."

Hans took a long draw of the Scotch as he stood up and turned toward a darkened window. Then, with his back still to Jon, he finally replied: "Okay, little brother. I'll go along on your word. But I want her out of here as soon as her husband's better or, more likely, at the first sign of trouble."

"There won't be any trouble."

"There's always trouble when it comes to Indians and women. You know that."

Jon's fist pounded the table rattling the Scotch glasses and scaring Fjord off into another room. "God-dammit, Hans," he was nearly shouting, "What are you talking about? There's been so few issues with the Ojibwa I can't even name one."

"I guess the bar fight over at Charlie's don't count." Hans moved about facing Jon, the power of his voice clashing with the anger in his brother's. "An Indian stabs and kills a white man over a woman he claimed belonged to him and you don't think that's trouble?"

"That was years ago, Hans. It's got nothing to do with this situation."

"I'm just sayin' trading with 'em is one thing. Letting one of their married women live in our house is another."

"Ojibwa women work as domestics all the time. She'll leave when he's back to work. You have my word." Jon was furious that he had to make his case. It reminded him of when they were boys back in Norway, and Hans always had the upper hand. *Hardheaded as hell,* he thought, *just like the old man.*

"I did the right thing," Jon pressed on, the agitation in his voice evening out. "My God, Hans, he was injured on our property. The least we can do is help 'em out and pay her to cook 'til he heals."

"I'm just sayin' what I said." Hans stood firm. "I won't bring it up again, but mark my words. There's almost always trouble when it comes to Indians and women, and you know it!" He threw back a final swig of his Scotch and picked up his empty plate, turning his back on Jon again as he moved toward the kitchen, his statement ringing loud and clear in every corner of the room.

"And I'm sayin' you can trust me on this." Jon was dug in as much, sticking with his gut, but with what he hoped was a lighter tactic. "When have you not been able to trust me?"

"I trust you Jon, but here's what I don't trust." Hans stopped and whirled around, glaring at his brother, repeating what he believed to be an irrefutable point. "She's young . . . she's Ojibwa . . . she's married, and as I'm sure you noticed, she's beautiful. When the trouble starts, I don't want flack over this. You hear me? She's gone. That's the deal. As soon as trouble hits—she's gone."

"Fine," said Jon, feeling the sting of his words and uncomfortable at the reference to her beauty. He didn't want to admit that Hans' words held truth and that he'd had his own reservations but that he couldn't help himself. How could he explain to his brother that he'd been spellbound by those eyes, that on the long ride back he'd been entranced by the deft way she'd handled her horse, by the way the light bounced off her long black hair, and by the faint scent of wildflower oil on her clothes? And so, he'd focused on the accident on Gustafson land, and trusted that, in spite of his reservations, Hans would see that they did owe her something, that letting her cook for them was the least they could do.

The floorboards creaked in the ceiling above them and a muffled *whoof* told them that Fjord was upstairs with Mahal as she readied herself for bed. The clock on the dining room mantle struck a chord. It was well past nine o'clock, late to be eating, and late to be having a serious conversation when worn out bodies and weary heads could distort the truth any which way.

CHAPTER SEVEN

By the time Christmas arrived that year, the tireless winds seemed to have blown themselves out, leaving the hills and fields shrouded in white as far as the eye could see. There was a sense of holiness in the empty, unspoiled land, in the vivid nights hung with stars, and in the air so cold and pure that one could imagine the breath of God himself.

"Mahal, look!" Jon threw a light snowball, rattling the kitchen window to get her attention. He had axed a young spruce tree and dragged it now across the floor, lacing the house with the scent of pine. The week before, he'd taught Mahal how to string popcorn he'd shaken over the fire. Now, rummaging through an old chest, Jon pulled out winsome homemade ornaments his mother had cherished through the years as well as the collection of small Norwegian flags she'd carried over on the boat, and he showed Mahal how to hang them all on the tree just the way his mother had liked it. "Not too close together," he told her, commenting on her choice of placement like a teacher doting on a pet pupil. And when she spaced one of the flags too high, he couldn't help but come up behind her and lower her arm. "Like this," he said, burning red just touching her, then catching himself and backing away. "See that. It's perfect now."

Mahal smiled shyly as they stood back to admire their handiwork. "It's beautiful," she said when the last of the colorful flags had gone up.

Her genuine statement filled him with happiness. Until now, Jon hadn't known how a simple task like twirling a strand of popcorn around a tree could bring him so much pleasure. He imagined himself with her, as if they were a married couple and this was their home.

"But not as beautiful as you," he smiled. He wanted her to know how much joy she had brought him by being there with him, but then, embarrassed by his boldness, he said: "Hey, I have a great idea. Let's ride up the mountain."

They took their time winding their horses up the broad side of Spirit Mountain, ethereal, wrapped in a winter landscape that held a life of it's own. It was easy to get lost in the sights and sounds of nature and the abundant winter wildlife that called the mountainside home. Birds sprang off silver branches, their chatter sprinkling the air. Rabbits, foxes, even wolves could be sighted darting behind trees, while hawks swooped down for the voles and the mice that scurried beneath the snow, and it seemed as if they spotted deer around every turn.

"Maybe I can catch us dinner," said Jon when they came upon a young buck who was resting beneath a nearby evergreen. Jon lifted his bow to take the shot, but a springy snowshoe rabbit caused the horses to shift, and his arrow missed his mark badly and lodged into the trunk of a dense pine. They watched as the frightened buck leapt off into the woods, his hind legs kicking up tufts of snow in his wake.

"Good," Mahal laughed, "I didn't want you to hit him."

"I thought you would be a natural hunter, Mahal," Jon said, dismounting his horse, kicking at the snow on his way to dislodge the arrow from the body of the tree. He smiled on the way back thinking about how nice it was that Mahal enjoyed riding with him on these increasingly frequent occasions and how different she was from a girl he'd once brought out from the city for a weekend. The girl had been afraid of horses and had politely declined his invitation to ride.

"When we're low on game, I'm as much a hunter as anyone," said Mahal. "But, we still have plenty of venison back at the house. Today the beauty of the animals in their natural home is more than enough."

Taking it slow halfway up the side of the mountain, Jon led them to a small overhang where they could look out over the valley below. "The first time I came up here with my father and brothers my dad told us a story about this mountain," said Jon gazing out across the expansive, tranquil land that spread wide and seemed to have no end.

"There are so many stories," said Mahal. "Which one did he tell you?"

Jon let his thoughts flow, happy to be able to recall for Mahal the first Indian folklore tale he'd ever heard. "A young, motherless Indian boy went out with his father, who was intent on teaching his son to be a great hunter," he began. "It was beautiful like today with the sun glistening on the snow and no winds disturbing the peaceful surroundings; only the chirping of the birds in the trees. Soon they had more than they needed—a deer, many rabbits and even a fox. So many that they had to load their bounty onto skins and pull it behind their horses.

"Though they had enough, when they came upon a set of wolf tracks in the snow, the boy's father pulled to a halt. 'I must have the wolf,' he said. 'It will make a great coat.'

"'We already have more than we need, father,' the boy replied.

"But the father shook his head and pressed on. Before long, the tracks led them to a she-wolf and a den of pups. 'Please don't kill me,' the mother wolf begged them. 'You have enough, and if I die, my pups will die too. There will be no one to hunt for them and to keep them warm.'

"But the boy's father, driven by his greed and the easy prey, raised up his bow to take aim. Before he could fire the arrow, however, a great gray wolf swooped out of nowhere onto his back, killing him instantly. The wolves feasted on the bounty the boy and his father had hunted, giving thanks to the dead animals' spirits for their nourishment, and when they were full, they shared what was left. Every animal on the mountain that night slept with a full belly.

"'Are you going to kill and eat me, too?' The boy was frightened that he would die as his father had. The gray wolf stepped forward.

"'No,' he said. 'There is no need to take more than our survival requires. It is not your fault that your father was greedy and did not heed this law of nature.'

"The wolves raised him as their own after that, and the boy never did return to his tribe. They say he lives somewhere up here still. Many have spotted him during a full moon, out searching for greedy hunters who disregard the laws of nature. When he finds them, he pushes them off the side of the mountain to their deaths.

"The tribesmen searched until they came upon the body of his father, but the boy has never been found."

Jon paused and turned his head to search Mahal's face for a reaction, but she had her eyes set out over the distance, somewhere far away. After several minutes she finally spoke: "Many suffer when the laws of nature are broken," she said. "It is a lesson in many of our stories, but I've never heard it told that way before."

The afternoon sun had warmed large patches of virgin snow that shimmered on the steep mountain slopes like sheets of starched linen. They dismounted their horses to walk to another lookout point that was familiar to anyone who spent time on the mountain. As Jon gazed out over the valley below, he felt humbled by the wonderment in all that nature could provide. His family had come so far, but there was so much left to do, and it was up to him and Hans to keep it all going. It had been a rough year, and for the first time, he had a sense of how nice it was to share a view such as this, something he loved so much, with a woman who appreciated it as much as he did. Losing himself in the moment, he imagined for a second that he was kissing her.

"It's wonderful having you living with us," said Jon breaking out of his fantasy. He wished that he could explain how much her presence had cheered the dull house and made him want to get up in the morning just to see her face over a cup of hot coffee.

"Gustafson Corridor is a beautiful place," Mahal answered. "I can't imagine how anyone could want more than this."

"So, you're happy here then?"

"If happiness is a choice, as you are suggesting, then yes, I'm happy."

"I've never met anyone quite like you." Jon said warmly and he was filled with an even deeper longing when he met her smiling eyes in return. They spent another hour or so enjoying the view, pointing out sightings that caught their attention. It was a moment in time that Jon knew he would cherish forever, but as the sun began to cast shadows in places that were once brilliant, he knew their excursion was over.

"Guess we should be getting back. Chores wait for no man." He laughed a bit at his twist on this common adage and was pleased when Mahal laughed along with him. "Let's go," he said, turning his horse as Mahal nudged Wind to follow up behind him.

Jon retraced his steps back to the main trail, and they wound their horses down in silence, riding into the farmyard an hour later with the magic of the mountain still heavy in their veins.

CHAPTER EIGHT

The following afternoon, three days before Christmas, Sunday chores were disrupted by the sound of jingling sleigh bells and Bjorn shouting "Merry Christmas!" as he drove up the driveway showing off a new horse-drawn sled stuffed with his four oldest kids, minus a three year old back at the farmhouse who didn't want to leave his mother.

"Merry Christmas," they all shouted at once when they came to a stop in front of the homestead.

Hans had been working in the barn, and he slid open the door to see what all the commotion was about. "Hello!" he shouted and waved as he strolled across the farmyard.

"Well, well! What do we have here?" He leaned over the side of the open sled and peered into the fresh faces of his nieces and nephews who sat scrunched together with a large blanket draped over their laps. "This is some sled you've got here. Is this your Christmas present?"

"Yes, yes!" The children resounded in chorus.

"Well, if you hadn't grown so big since the last time I saw you, I'd jump in and have a ride, too."

"Do!" they shouted and waved toward the front door. "You too, Uncle Jon. Come ride with us!"

Jon was standing in his stocking feet with the door wide open waving hello. "What's all the racket about?" he yelled in a playful voice as Mahal stepped into view and handed him his coat and boots.

"Who's that?" the kids giggled and squirmed as their handsome uncle strode toward them with the air of a man who was happy to be alive. Bjorn's twelve-year-old twin girls were especially curious to know who this stranger was and what she was doing there.

"That's Mahal," said Jon stepping up and shaking hands with Bjorn. "Merry Christmas," he said to his brother before turning his attention to the kids. "She's come to cook for us."

"She's pretty." One of the girls giggled and Bjorn, from what he could see, couldn't help but notice that she was plenty young as well.

"Are you going to come for a ride with us?" The kids wouldn't let up.

"You're too big," said Hans in an affectionate and teasing way. "There's no room!"

"Ahhhhh," they acquiesced with big sighs. "We hardly ever get to see you."

"Oh, yeah! Well, why don't you come over for Christmas Eve dinner then?"

"That's a great idea, Hans," Jon broke in, turning to Bjorn. "Why don't you bring Jorunn and the kids and come over for dinner Wednesday night," he said. "I'll heat up a stockpot of Pa's glogg and ask Mahal to cook the lutefisk we've been saving for a special occasion. Tell Emil to come too and show off his baby. I hear Marga's got her hands full. I'm sure she could use a night off."

"Sounds good," answered Bjorn, stepping up into the driver's seat. "I'll get Jorunn to make one of her spiced-apple pies."

"Come around four o'clock," said Jon. He and Hans backed away from the sled as Bjorn picked up the reins, letting them know that he was ready to go. "We'll see you then."

"Will do." Bjorn shouted over his shoulder as the horses lurched forward and the sled, full of the exuberant waving children, slid away.

In times past, when their parents were still alive, they would all have been together on Christmas day, but now, nearly a full year after their deaths, not a word had been spoken and formal plans had not been made. A party on Christmas Eve to bring them all together seemed perfect.

Wednesday rolled around and nine Gustafson grandchildren, ranging in age from thirteen to Emil's not yet one-year-old baby, burst through the formal entrance that Jon had draped with branches of evergreen and holly, the red berries as decorative as the beads woven through Mahal's dreamcatcher. The old house had felt lighter and more cheerful after Jon and Mahal had decorated the tree, but now with all of these bodies running about the atmosphere was positively joyful, and it vibrated with the bustle and energy of their young spirits to such an extent that it almost felt like old times. Jon and Mahal spread a lace runner end-to-end between them and placed it on the side-table in the dining room, setting out glass mugs for the glogg, a hot mulled red wine steeped with sugar and cardamom, cinnamon, cloves, and bitter orange. Bjorn's wife, Jorunn, and Emil's wife, Marga, pitched in, setting out serving platters and a set of linen napkins that Marga had stitched for her mother-in-law before she died. Soon plates of raisins and blanched almonds appeared to accompany the glogg, as well as hot chocolate and a piled-high plate of ginger cookies for the kids.

The atmosphere was festive and party-like with the women busy in the kitchen and chasing after the scattering kids. It had been more than a year since any of them had been together like this, and everyone caught a bit of the old Christmas spirit. After they'd all had several rounds, Jon pulled a pint of aquavit down from a wall shelf next to the Christmas tree. "Try a bit of this," he said and tipped it into the mugs, laughing it up with his brothers who were slowly growing inebriated on their own and hardly needed anymore help. Indulging in the spirits loosened up their otherwise stoic composures, and none was more affected than Jon who seemed determined to drink himself free of his inhibitions.

As the afternoon wore on, his compulsions knew fewer and fewer boundaries. It became increasingly less and less possible for him to keep his focus off of Mahal, who was polite to the group but preferred to keep herself separated and busy in the kitchen.

"Mahal," he called out, slurring his words a bit when he realized she wasn't in the parlor where they had all managed to gather. "Come on in here and admire the tree with us!"

Before any of them knew it, Jon was leading Mahal by the hand into the crowded room where Bjorn, Emil, and the two sisters-in-law eyed her with suspicion and were more than a little anxious to know her story. Upon arriving, they had expected a cook, a servant really, and were surprised when she was not dressed as such, though Mahal had spent the majority of the afternoon keeping her distance and focusing her attention on the preparations. Now, Jon was pulling her into their midst as if she were a guest of great importance.

At first, Mahal had been excited at Jon's insistence that she wear her best dress, but her enthusiasm turned to embarrassment when she saw how different she looked from the other women. Mahal, with silver earrings dangling against her light brown skin, wore a dark blue dress that looked deep and rich, with the edges trimmed in her own colorful beadwork. She appeared exotic and rendered an ornateness that so contrasted the plain, pale faces and unadorned dresses of the brothers' wives that her presence left them more than a little uncomfortable. The way the dress hugged her breasts and accented her small waist did not go unnoticed either by Jorunn, who was more than a little plump after birthing five children, or Marga who was still breast feeding and had not lost her baby weight after delivering her fourth. Beaded clothing and dangling jewelry were not familiar items in their world where function took precedence over adornment, and they found it disconcerting to be confronted with something that they had deemed "superficial" at a family Christmas gathering such as this.

Oblivious as to how Mahal's appearance was being received, Jon scanned the room for a comfortable chair. "Shoo," he said to two of the smaller kids nestled in one of the club chairs near the fire. He settled Mahal into the chair, pressing a mug of the hot glogg into her hands.

"Have a sip." He waited like an anxious parent to read the expression on her face as she reluctantly took a sip of the spicy wine. "Do you like it?"

Her mouth puckered at the corners. "I would have to get used to it," she said, shyly, dropping her eyes.

It was Emil's wife, Marga, who took it upon herself to ask the questions she knew they were all curious to know the answers to.

"Where are you from, Mahal?" she began. Marga was settled on the parlor room davenport with her baby on her lap next to Jorrun who loved a full view of the fire. "Where is your family?"

"I'm from Red Lake," Mahal answered, timidly, "but my people now live on the reservation in Fond du Lac."

"Your people? Do you mean your parents?"

"My parents are gone a long while now. I mean the Ojibwa. My mother-in-law is there and my . . . husband."

"Husband? Children too? My goodness, what are you doing here in Gustafson Corridor?"

"No," Mahal shook her head. "There are no children."

Jon, ever protective of Mahal, stepped in then, attempting to rescue her from a conversation that was veering into dangerous territory.

"Her husband was injured on our land up north, so we're helping out by employing her 'til he heals," Jon pronounced, anxious to dispel any ideas that Mahal was in their midst for any other reason other than that the family owed her something. But the women were anxious to hear from Mahal herself and, half ignoring Jon's defense, kept their focus so intently on Mahal that she felt compelled to respond.

"Yes, my husband was nearly killed when a stack of logs let loose," Mahal said, her eyes dropping again to her lap, her quiet voice in distinct contrast to the skeptical group and boisterous children. "His back was injured, and it is difficult for him to work."

"Oh, that's terrible." Marga commiserated, but her eyebrows raised up at this new revelation: Mahal was married. Neither Jon nor Hans had mentioned a word about her marital status, and it had never occurred to any of them that she wasn't single. As a matter of fact, before they had arrived that afternoon, they hadn't given much thought to the news that a cook had been hired and moved in. The children had said she was "pretty," but now Mahal was proving to be so much more than pretty, and her stunning good looks certainly did not fit their image of a woman who was "just a cook."

"I don't know a man alive who doesn't need help around a house," said Jorunn. "But all the same, as a married woman, I'm sure you're anxious to get back to your family." There was a disapproving tone in her voice that was not lost on either Mahal or Jon, and when Marga jumped in, the judgment in the air was almost palpable.

"Yes," she agreed and stood up to hand the baby off to her husband, preventing him from ladling another mug of glogg. "I, for one, can't imagine being away from Emil for any length of time, especially if he was injured." She put an emphasis on the word, "especially," in a way that underlined the critical tone of Jorunn's comment.

"Maybe there is work closer to Fond du Lac," said Hans, suddenly buoyed up by this voicing of support for the feelings he'd been harboring since the day he'd come home and found Mahal in the kitchen. "I'm sure it'd be nice to ride home every night instead of being stuck out here with the likes of us all week."

Jon gulped his drink and re-ladled, dropping in a pinch of raisins from a side plate. Hans' comment infuriated him, but he struggled to hold it together. "Well, for now she's not going anywhere," he said, his anger evident in his flushed, red face. "You know it's Hans and I who are the lucky ones. I've already packed on a few pounds with Mahal's good cooking, and as far as I'm concerned she's welcome to stay as long as she likes."

"I'll ask around in town," said Hans, ignoring his brother's remarks with an obliging slap to Jon's back and a nod toward Mahal who sat rooted in her chair, desperately wishing she could return to the safety of the kitchen.

The moony look on Jon's face when he spoke of Mahal and his anger over the slightest suggestion that she should go elsewhere was duly noted by all, and the scene set eyes rolling, especially Jorunn and Marga, who had never witnessed any tension between the brothers before.

Their questions had initially stemmed from little more than polite curiosity, but the more they learned, the more they wondered what Jon's intentions toward Mahal were and what it might mean for the family. And, while they did not doubt the veracity of what they'd been told, Jon's erratic behavior and the tension with Hans watered seeds of doubt that Mahal's presence could ever be a good thing.

As the evening wore on, Jon found it more and more challenging to ignore their furtive glances and whispered remarks, but in spite of it all, he kept himself close to Mahal who seemed to shrink deeper and deeper into her chair. When one of the older children who had taken the baby from Emil's arms suddenly stepped around and plopped him into Mahal's lap, she perked up a bit and quietly bounced him on her knee as he reached for her long, silver earrings, swinging like shiny toys off the ends of her ears.

"Let's serve dinner, Mahal," said Jon when little Harald began fussing and his mother slipped him from Mahal's lap.

Jon took Mahal's hand and helped her out of the chair and she followed him into the kitchen. They had not been out of earshot for more than a minute, when tongues started wagging.

"I wonder if she shares in his affections?" whispered Marga in a low voice, patting the baby's back to hush him. She watched as Jorunn scrambled toward the fireplace where her three year old had wandered too close.

"She's so quiet it's hard to say," Jorunn answered leading her small son back to the davenport and hefting him onto her lap.

"Well, she seems to follow him—does whatever he asks her to do." Marga shifted her baby to her other shoulder where he seemed to be more comfortable.

"Ma and Pa are gone n'aer a year and look what happens," said Jorunn. "If Pa were here, he'd never 'a let her in the house."

Marga carefully shifted her weight toward the warmth of the burning logs so as not to disturb her now quiet son. "Pa'd say it isn't proper. He would have talked some sense into Jon long before this."

"Well, it isn't proper, is it?" Jorunn responded. "I'm just not sure what anyone can do about it at this point."

"Hans, can't you talk some sense into your brother?" Marga shifted her attention to her brother-in-law and raised her voice to make sure he would hear her.

As if on cue, Jon poked his head in from the dining room before Hans could respond. "Dinner's ready!" he called. "Come and get it while everything's still hot."

"I've tried, but he won't listen." Hans impatiently answered his sister-in-law and then hurried off to the dining room, unwilling to be pulled into the conversation.

Marga and Jorunn exchanged a look that communicated their shared concern as Marga stood up to carry the now sleeping boy to a small crib they had set up in a warm nook where he would not be disturbed. "Maybe things'll look different with full bellies."

Jon and Mahal had set up the food, buffet style, on the old oak dining room table, the lutefisk smothered with bits of thick, chopped bacon, overcooked peas and potatoes, and plates of bread with cold cuts. Steaming macaroni and cheese had been set out for the younger ones who pinched their noses at the pungent fish.

Hans piled his plate high and distanced himself from Jon by perching on the opposite end of the long table, and as he ate, he ruminated about the flirtatious nature of Jon's interactions with Mahal all evening. He knew the glogg had a way of going to one's head. Maybe it had caused Jon to think he was in love. Things would look different in the morning, he told himself.

When the meal was over and the bickering of the children signaled it was time to go home, the wives carried plates and packed up leftovers as they buzzed around Mahal in the kitchen and urged their older children to help the younger ones tug on mittens and hats. Before the baby was bundled and the last scarf had been tied, Jon was splayed out on the davenport sound asleep. The younger children paraded past him finding it hysterical that they could not wake him no matter how loudly they yelled: "Goodbye, Uncle Jon." The families uttered polite "goodbyes" to Mahal, who remained ensconced in the kitchen dutifully scrubbing up the remnants of the gathering. Hans followed them out the door, preferring to say his farewell to Bjorn and Emil in private. Sensing this, the women moved the children ahead and the brothers took a minute for themselves.

"What's going on with Jon?" Emil asked him. "I'm still not sure I have the whole story about the Ojibwa woman, but he sure seems determined to keep her around."

"I don't know what's got into him," Hans said, with a shake of his head. "Jon thinks we owe her 'cause her husband was injured on our land. I was against her coming here. You know how people talk. He won't listen to reason. So far that's about all there is to it, but it's nothing I'll ever be comfortable with."

"Well, it's been a rough year," Bjorn answered, uneasy with meddling in anyone's business, let alone that which involved his younger brothers. "I'm sure the woman will be back on the reservation sooner rather than later. Sometimes a man has to let off a little steam. Jon probably won't remember talkin' so much when he wakes up."

"I hope you're right," Hans replied. "I'll be in touch."

On his way back into the house Hans loaded his arms with wood from the porch and dropped it in the kitchen near the hearth, brushing off his hands and rinsing them in the sink. "Looks like Jon's going to sleep it off in the parlor tonight," he said to Mahal. "I say we just let him be."

Things were spiraling beyond his control faster than Hans could ever have predicted. Jon was falling hard for this woman and acting like a fool to boot. "That woman could never be his," Hans muttered, but even as he uttered this assurance to himself, he wondered where all of this was leading and what, if anything, he should do about it. Hans splashed himself a Dewar's and retired to Jon's study to mull it over. He cracked a window, allowing a fresh stream of air to permeate the room. Sinking back into a soft leather chair, Hans propped his legs up on the white oak desk his father had built and allowed his mind to wander to happier memories. One of the first stories he and Jon heard when they arrived from Norway was how their father had spent weeks carving and polishing this desk after long, grueling days in the fields. His father had been able to speak and read English before any of them, and no one they knew could match his stamina for all things related to work. He had chopped the wood and built it with his own hands long before they had a dining room table. Emil joked that they'd eaten so many meals on it, it reeked of gravy and spilt milk.

"If I'm going to do business and succeed in America, I must have a proper desk," his father had insisted, and Hans remembered the way he would sit there moving a dim oil lamp over newspapers and local journals, scribbling notes in the margins as he read. Resting there like that, Hans thought about how much the desk reminded him of his father and how much he loved the wood, for its strength and the beauty of its rich, warm color. He ran his hand over the varnished top that was now an heirloom and would be passed down through the generations. The brothers had opted to leave it in the main house, but in the future it would go to Bjorn's oldest son, James.

It was almost impossible for Hans to imagine himself with children. He'd never been in a relationship. He didn't know what it meant to answer to a woman that way, to go through life tied to one person who expected things from you, depended on you. He'd been to bars in the west end of Duluth, slept with a few women those rare times when he'd felt inclined to do so, but they were hard, smoky women that frequented those kinds of places and who always had a room to go off to before morning. He never had much to say to them, and he'd certainly never been in love. As far as he knew, Jon had never been in love either, but now here he was acting almost like a stranger around a woman who couldn't have been a more unlikely candidate.

A deep chill ran down Hans' back, and he pushed the window down part way just as he thought he heard footsteps in the parlor room. He pushed himself up from his chair and walked lightly down the short hallway to the doorway of the parlor in time to watch Mahal lay an Indian blanket over Jon. For one instant, Mahal's eyes met Hans' glare, but she quickly turned to go and Hans retreated back to the study letting the door swing closed behind him.

CHAPTER NINE

Slowly, as the Christmas season faded and the days and weeks drew on, with her tasks at hand and no further talk of her situation, Mahal gained a sense of purpose and established a pattern to her days. She awoke at dawn, stoked the fire, and laid out plates of lefse, the doughy flatbread that Jon and Hans liked to roll up for breakfast along with an assortment of cold meats and cheese. After the brothers left for the day, Mahal spent most of her time in the kitchen, cleaning up after one meal and preparing the next, aware by now of the likes and dislikes of each of the men and anxious to cater to both. Sometimes she'd sit at the table and practice her handwriting on a tablet Jon had left for her, or browse through a Ladies magazine he thought she might enjoy. Jon was friendly and willing, shuttling logs from the wood shed to the porch, offering her peppermint Life Savers and chewing gum, complimenting her on her cooking, even sharing books with her he thought she'd find interesting.

"See this," he said, hoisting one of his horticulture books onto the kitchen table and pointing out page after page of beautiful hand-drawn illustrations of tender, ripe vegetables so colorful and real Mahal thought she could almost pick them up off the page and eat them. "I'm going to plant a garden this spring and you'll be able to go out and *shop* for fresh vegetables just by walking out the door," he laughed, and she smiled broadly in return at the prospect.

Once, he dropped a handful of fortune cookies on the kitchen table on a day he'd been to town. "Pick one," he insisted, and they broke them all open, reading every fortune until they got one they both liked. "Today will be your lucky day," it read, and Mahal laughed at such a notion.

Yesterday, he'd teased her to laughing when she jumped at the pop-up toaster he'd ordered from the Sears catalog. Fjord flirted shamelessly also, trailing her like an eight-week-old puppy, tugging at her skirts and having to be sweet-talked out of the kitchen when Jon wanted his company on a trip to town.

Hans, on the other hand, stayed clear and remote, jealous over Jon's flirtations and the seeming ease at which his brother was able to get Mahal to loosen up. The way Jon looked at her when she tied up her skirt to sweep the floor or braided up her hair revealing the tawny nape of her neck did not go unnoticed either. And then there was the time when Mahal had tip-toed down the squeaky kitchen stairs after the brothers had retired for the night, filled a galvanized tub with hot water and slipped into her bath. Hans had heard the metal scraping on the linoleum floor and the kettles of hot water as they filled the tub. In an uncharacteristic moment of curiosity, he stepped silently into the door of the dining room. There he glimpsed her through the fire that burned low between the rooms, lying back with her eyes closed, her breasts exposed in the water, her loose hair barely grazing the floor. He had never witnessed a woman this way before, so primal and self-contained. *She is so beautiful*, he thought as an equally primal stirring ran through his body. *So fragile and vulnerable.* He couldn't help himself from staring at her between the dancing flames, his heart pounding; the palms of his hands growing damp. Finally, he forced himself to turn away. "The girl shouldn't be here," he grumbled, angry at himself for allowing such an indulgence. "She belongs to somebody else."

The next day, with images of Mahal's naked body haunting him and threatening to cloud every thought, Hans rode his horse into Duluth after he and his foreman had spent the morning drawing up plans for spring crops and eighty acres of new land that would be configured into their holdings. Drake's secretary, Irma, a middle-aged widow who was constantly tying up Drake's phone line gossiping with her church friends waved him in. He found Drake slouched over his work, the iconic duck-headed walking stick propped in its usual place alongside his desk.

"Hey, Ramsey," Hans called out as he stuck his head inside the doorway of Drake's dusty office.

"Hello, Hans. How are you? I darn near forgot you were comin' in today." He yanked a file out from under a tall stack of papers. "You know the mill's verbally accepted your offer on the open land, and I know I got your check here somewhere. Jon's already signed the formal offer. Now I need your signature, and I can get this over to them. How soon do you want to close?"

"As soon as possible," said Hans. "Any word from the bank?"

"Bank's all lined up. We should be ready to move ahead as soon as this offer comes back."

The brothers had bid on a large tract of farmland near the town of Cloquet, situated on the St. Louis River. The town had been ravaged by a fire two years prior, but was now flourishing in a frenzy to rebuild. A prosperous farmer was eager to sell off portions of his land that had made it through unscathed. The railroad had augmented the logging business there, so it looked like a solid investment. The brothers' forays up north had opened doors for further opportunities, and when word had come down about the land sale, they had pounced.

"Ah, here it is," Drake opened a manila file and lifted a document from the top of the stack. "Sign right here. You know you're gettin' a hell of a deal. I'd buy it myself if I could get the money."

"We're excited about this one," Hans responded, scribbling his name on the document and making a joke. "Jon's masterful at finding the deals. He always seems to know the best time to move. Sometimes I think he's got access to classified real estate information. You know, the secret stuff."

"Well, speaking of Jon, I know you weren't too keen on his hirin' that Ojibwa woman to cook for you. Just so happens, I might have solution for that, too."

"What do you mean?" said Hans, surprised, but hesitant. This was not a subject he had planned on discussing with Drake.

"Well, let me start off by saying that I don't like meddling, Lord knows, but I told your Pa I'd look after you boys, and this situation you got with the Indian woman is concerning. There's been some talk around town about it lately, the missus says, and that's never good for business. A married woman alone with two young men certainly doesn't look right, and it sounds like Jon is somewhat smitten. I sure would hate to see him get into any trouble."

"I agree," interjected Hans.

"I thought of something," Drake told him. "There's a lot of hustle over in Cloquet right now. A good chunk of the town sits on the reservation. A good friend of mine runs Northwest Paper, and he's got a handful of kids and a weary wife. Told me last week he's lookin' for some extra help. I thought of your situation right away. I think they'd take your Ojibwa woman, providing she's willing to do the cooking and help with five small children. I know your woman's good. Hell, Jon can't say enough about her." Drake smiled wryly, knowing he had struck a chord with Hans. He knew how much Hans had disapproved of the situation from the beginning.

Hans stood up and walked to the window taking up the duck-carved walking cane and drew back the curtain the way he had seen Drake do several times before. The sky was blue and cloudless, and as long as he didn't look down upon the train platform and all the snow that still covered the ground, he thought that it could have been summer. "I appreciate your concern, Drake," he continued after a moment, "but there's no need to do that."

"What do you mean?" Drake's chair swiveled around as he cleared his throat to avoid one of his dry coughing spells. He scrounged around the menagerie of papers and files searching for a handkerchief, which he finally pulled out from under a heavy law book and held to his mouth as a precaution. "If she worked in Cloquet there'd be no excuse for her not to be with her family. It could be a good situation for all concerned, especially you."

"Yes," Hans agreed, moving back to his seat and setting the cane back in its regular spot alongside Drake's desk. "It would have been the perfect solution when she first hired on, but Jon's been busy lately. He's not been paying her any mind. The word is that her husband's nearly healed too, so I don't expect her to be around much longer. Might as well let it be."

If Drake saw through Hans' lie, he didn't show it. "Well, then," he said, sticking the wadded handkerchief back under the book. "It appears that the problem has worked itself out. I'm glad to hear it. I'll have my courier get these papers over to the mill today. You'll be hearing from me before too long, I'm sure."

Hans was surprised by how relieved he felt that Drake had turned his attention back to business. He justified his lie by telling himself that as much as he would like Mahal gone, this was just not a good time to be upsetting things at home. *This is our biggest business deal since selling the stumpage rights on the standing timber up north*, he thought. *What would be the point of upsetting Jon now?*

Out in the street, dark lines of tracks were slow to melt and visible in the hard-packed snow where the trolleys made a rusty crawl, their only cure being a vat of oil. It was mid-March, and there were still plenty of clumps of brown snow on the streets, but, it was a cloudless sky. The sun blazed high ending a long stretch of bleak days with little light.

Hans took his time riding home. Every now and then they'd get a day like today—fifty degrees in March—and he was ready to wrap up the long winter and get into spring planting, but Hans could hardly enjoy the mild weather. He was too preoccupied with the conversation he'd had with Drake. He vacillated between trying to convince himself of the validity of his own excuse for keeping Mahal in the house to thinking that maybe he should have let Drake go ahead with his plan to find her another job. He was concerned about how often the vision of Mahal in her bath floated into his thoughts, as he struggled to solve an issue at work or fall asleep after a hard day. Now, here he was, making excuses to keep her longer. *What is wrong with me?* he admonished himself. *We should definitely let her go.* But he knew deep down that he wouldn't change his mind, and he shook it off as he galloped his horse toward home.

When Hans trotted into the farmyard an hour later he found the chores had already been tended to by young Finn, the neighbor boy they'd hired on. Jon's quarter horse was in his stall bedded down with blankets and nibbling on a manger of oats. There was one extra stall in the barn, which Hans had planned on filling with a stud horse that summer to breed with his mare, but, Jon had given the stall to Mahal's horse, Wind, who raised his eyes for a moment as if to verify that the plan would have to change. Hans took his time brushing down his horse, letting his thoughts settle before he refilled a milk pan for the barn cats and treated them to a fistful of kibble that he made by crushing grain with the dried beef stored in an old rain barrel.

Lights from the house windows looked welcoming at the end of the day, and when he entered the kitchen, he found Mahal up to her wrists in a bowl of dough. She looked up, startled, but quickly averted her eyes after a quiet greeting when she saw that it was Hans. Fjord, resting in his familiar spot by the fire, got up to greet Hans, and Hans returned the favor with a brisk pat on the head.

"Where's Jon?" he asked her, catching his coat on a wall peg. "I saw his horse in the barn." He had become used to seeing Jon in the kitchen with Mahal. Many times Jon had moved his paperwork from the study and spread it out on the kitchen table so that he could be near Mahal.

"Yes, he's here," she said and for a moment she ceased her kneading, and they faced each other in a rare exchange. "He's back in his study."

Hans stomped off with Fjord in his wake. "Hey," he said bracing his arms in the doorway to Jon's study.

"Hi," Jon dropped his ink pen and glanced up from his ledger. "What's going on?"

"Talked to Drake today," said Hans.

"Oh yeah. Did you sign the offer?"

"I signed, and he said they've accepted verbally already, so it looks like we've got a deal. He'll call us when he gets the papers back, sometime near the end of the week."

"Well, it's never a done deal until everybody's signed, but you're right, it looks good."

"Drake said the bank's good too, so we can go to closing anytime after that."

"It'll go fast, now. When are you free to head over there?"

"How about Friday? I got Arvin Park's son riding over from Proctor in the morning to chop the wood we got piled up behind the barn, but once I've got him squared away we can head out."

"That would work," Jon answered. "When Drake calls we can let him know we agree on Friday, sometime before noon if that works for them."

"Sounds good," said Hans before heading back to his room to change.

Thirty minutes later Mahal appeared in the doorway of Jon's study. "Dinner is ready," she said.

Jon's face lit up, and he abandoned his deskwork immediately to join her in the hallway. "I'm starving," he said. "Hans!" he yelled. "Come on, dinner's ready."

In the weeks that Mahal had been at the house, Jon had invited her to join them in the dining room for supper rather than eat off by herself in the kitchen. Now three places were always set, and they took their meals together. After supper and before dishes though, Mahal would always excuse herself to go out to the barn to brush down Wind.

"She sure does love that horse," said Hans when he heard the kitchen door close and was certain that she had gone.

Jon glanced at Hans, surprised at what he'd heard. It was the first nice comment Jon had heard his brother make about Mahal since she'd arrived in Gustafson Corridor.

"She sure does," Jon answered. "If anyone could understand that, it'd be you. I can't think of anyone other than you who loves horses more than Mahal does." He watched as Hans tasted a sip of his coffee then added a touch of cream. "And you've got to admit she's a great cook. Hasn't been any trouble either. Am I right that you're feeling better about the whole situation?"

"Haven't given it much thought one way or another," Hans replied, "but I guess the time will come when her husband's healed up, and that'll be that, just like you said in the beginning." He looked down into his cup and saucer, pretending the coffee needed sugar and swirled in a teaspoonful. He'd never concealed anything from his brother before, but after the clumsy fib he'd told Drake he was self conscious and eager to end the conversation.

"I never saw you take sugar in your coffee before," said Jon, off-handedly setting his cup and saucer on his empty dessert plate and making his way into the kitchen.

Jon had thought a lot about what was said at the Christmas gathering by his sisters-in-law and reaffirmed by Hans. Of course, they were right. Mahal was a married woman, and she deserved to be close to her family. And yet when he imagined life without her, he admitted to himself that he loved her more than he had ever loved anyone before.

Every week Jon made efforts to ease the burdens of Mahal's life as if doing so might shake her resolve to ride to the reservation the next weekend. No matter how hard he tried to make her feel at home and welcome though, to make her feel special and even doted upon, she kept religiously to her obligations, riding Wind back to Fond du Lac. Jon always sensed an urgency in her preparations to leave, like a child who might be punished if she didn't do what was expected, and the concerns he harbored about possible abuse troubled him all weekend.

He gnawed on the situation, constantly playing the possibilities over in his mind, coming to no definitive conclusions. Every time he thought of Mahal returning to a man who could not control his anger, he became upset. The whole thing sent Jon into a mood that didn't go unnoticed by Hans. On Friday afternoons, when Jon heard her unlatch the kitchen door, he'd move to the window of his small study and watch her speaking softly to Wind, as she led him into the yard from his stall in the barn. Sunday nights she returned, sullen and revealing nothing about her other life. Jon thought that her husband's health must be improving though, because the previous week when she returned, he'd noticed a small cut on her lip. Jon had said nothing, and the new week had begun with him going out of his way once again to gain her trust and her affection.

PART TWO
THE BLIZZARD

CHAPTER TEN

The front that blew across the prairie on a dull, cheerless Tuesday almost four months after Mahal's arrival had not been predicted. No Farmer's Almanac had picked it up. No early freezes or atypical snows had given any indication that this winter would be any different from the infinite number before it. Though the weather had been bitterly cold again, Jon had not thought twice before taking the wagon into town for supplies and casual business that morning, mustering Fjord onto the seat beside him. Hans had left on a scouting run three days prior and, for the most part, it was business as usual. Mahal would have thought nothing about it either had she not taken note of the sky, a phantom of gray-white light, painful to the eye in its eerie brightness and punctuated by dark clouds hovering low over a wavy tree line in the distance. Stepping out for kindling, she paused for a breath of the artic-like air, wary of the brooding sky and sensing the danger she suspected was lurking there. The quiet moment was broken only by a flock of ducks honking overhead, fleeing into the lonely wilderness. She shielded her eyes with her hand, squinting after the ducks until they'd all but disappeared, and the stillness returned.

The morning felt as long and vast as the sky and dragged on endlessly for Mahal. She had become accustomed to the shadowing of Fjord most days, who was more than happy to keep her company. Having set a stew to simmer, she began folding cinnamon into rice pudding near noon when the sky went strangely dark, the wind kicked up, and snow devils, like small angry tornados, whirled through the farmyard followed by heavy flurries that left the air as dusty as a sack of flour. The temperature plunged so drastically that Mahal dropped everything to shuttle in an armful of wood and stoke up the fire. By late afternoon, only shadowy glimpses of the big red barn were visible from the kitchen window. When Mahal realized that Finn would not show up for chores in a storm like this, she bundled up and moved Wind and the four other horses from the corral into the barn, straining against the stiff gusts to slide the heavy barn door shut before making a dash back to the warmth and safety of the farmhouse. The thick snow had already drifted near the troublesome kitchen door, and she kicked at it, wrestling another load of wood into the house, stumbling forward as it tumbled from her arms to the floor near the hearth. Taking a minute to catch her breath, Mahal worried that perhaps Jon might have trouble making it home. Random thoughts like this began to race through her mind as the overhead bulb flickered, threatening to kill the precious light and spiking a good dose of fear in her heart. Seconds later, as if on cue, pellets of ice blistered the windows and rattled the wood-framed panes, threatening the glass.

When it was long past the supper hour and still no sign of the men, Mahal sat alone at the kitchen table picking at the stew she'd been simmering all day as the house creaked and moaned, straining itself against the now raging blizzard like a wooden dyke about to burst. Surrounded by the sounds of an impending disaster, she recalled the time when, as a young girl of four or five, a fierce and unpredicted hailstorm had collapsed a wall of the teepee she shared with her mother. She had been certain they were going to die, and that same feeling returned to her now.

Mahal liked to think of herself as a calm, brave person but the reverberating noise, the timbre of the wind, so ghostly and threatening, were almost more than she could bear. Struggling to calm herself, she rested close to the warmth of the fire, telling herself that the storm would blow over soon, and that she had nothing to fear. Momentarily calmed, she returned to the tasks of the kitchen and the comfort that she found in bringing order to what she had come to consider her domain.

Just as she began to dry the dishes, however, her fraying demeanor was shattered by a loud crash of breaking glass. Terrified, Mahal screamed and rushed into the parlor where the wind had hurled a thick branch into the window, smashing out the panes. The splintered tree branch, wet with ice and snow, stuck halfway into the room as if it were a spear that had been pitched by a hunter determined to make his mark. Mahal frantically searched for something to shove into the sides of the fractured window to plug the gaps and keep the frigid air from further compromising her already precarious situation. When the animal rug from in front of the fireplace proved to be too cumbersome, she retrieved a stack of Indian blankets from the kitchen and pushed them into the space around the top and sides of the giant limb. She cut her hand on a shard of jagged glass as she worked, but she ignored it, more concerned with how long the blankets would stay put before the wind blew them out again. With Mahal's nerves now as shattered as the glass and her bleeding hand wrapped up in the skirt of her apron, she closed off the door to the room, rolling another rug against the bottom of the door to help stave off the draft.

She returned to the kitchen, but before she had time to tend to the cut on her hand, the lights flickered and the room went black. For several minutes Mahal scrambled, nervously lighting candles and a dusty oil lamp kept in the pantry for emergencies such as this. But the augmented light did not keep more anxiety from rising up inside her chest and challenging her usually serene nature. She held her injured hand under the faucet, but when she tried to wash her wound with cold running water, she found there was none, only the water left in the pipes that quickly slowed to a trickle before going completely dry. With Mahal's frustration and fear mounting, she tore a thin dishtowel in half and bound her hand tightly to stop the bleeding.

Where is Jon? she wondered. *He should have been home hours ago.* Too scared to retire to her room, Mahal huddled by the fire, fears of what might have happened to him and the eerie noises of the storm wreaking havoc on her mind. *Oh Great Spirit, whose voice I hear in the winds,* she prayed. *As one of your many children I come asking for your help. Please bring him home safely.*

Frustrated and shaken, Mahal flashed on another time in her life when she felt this kind of fear and helplessness, like at the age of fourteen when she and her mother had both come down with pneumonia, one of the deadly diseases brought in by the white settlers years before. The disease had crept through the reservation like a poisonous snake, striking one clan after the next. Drifting in and out of delirium, Mahal feared that the flesh-eating spirit, Windigo, who waited in the depths of the black winter woods for a taste of human meat, would find her and eat her alive. But after three days her fever broke, and the Ojibwa women who nursed her told her that she would live but that her mother's spirit was making the walk westward to the sacred land where souls dwell after death. Mahal had been engulfed by fear—fear of Windigo, fear of loneliness, fear of the future without her mother to care for her. Others in the tribe took her in and were kind to her, but Mahal was lost and desperate. She struggled to feel a part of this new family but in less than a year she'd been married off to a man in his twenties though she was not yet fifteen. Though considered an eligible and desirable man by other single women in the tribe, it wasn't long before she learned that her new husband possessed a fiery temper that frightened her. At times it felt as though she'd come face to face with Windigo himself.

When she finally got up the nerve, Mahal rummaged through the kitchen pantry for a box of candles and spotted two more dusty kerosene lanterns on a shelf that was too high to reach. Stacking a couple of potato crates she hefted them down, one by one, and in no time, the room was amply lit, and she felt comfortable enough to breath a sigh of relief.

An hour later, when she thought she heard the howl of a timber wolf, Mahal rushed to scrape the frosted kitchen window with a butter knife so that she could peer into the darkness. Off in the distance a specter-like figure emerged from the blur, and she realized with a quickening in her heart that the sound she'd heard was a man's voice muffled by the wind, urging his horse toward the barn. "Jon!" she cried, elated with joy, "Jon!" Wild with relief, Mahal thanked the Great Spirit for bringing him home safely. Ten minutes later the snow-encrusted figure trudged through the kitchen door clawing back the snow that had, by now, piled up halfway to the doorknob.

Grateful that he had made it home alive and desperate for the comfort of company, Mahal clambered to his aid. Clumps of snow clung to his eyelashes and to the bits of hair exposed at the edges of his big fur hat. He stomped his boots and shoved back his hat, spraying Mahal with snow and beads of slush, and then she realized with a start, that it was Hans who had made it safely through the storm. Still, she struggled to be of use, tugging frozen chunks of ice off his face and yanking the stiff leather gloves off his hands. When Hans was able to clear his throat enough to speak, she recognized the hollow unfamiliar look of fear in his eyes and that his face bore the expression of one who had managed to escape a close brush with death.

"Broke camp . . . this . . . morning," he hung his head, wheezing, finding it difficult to make his lips form the letters. His mouth was so stiff with cold that all he could do was stammer one or two words with each labored breath. "Rode clear of the muskegs and bogs . . . fightin' the weather."

Mahal steered Hans close to the fire, where he shed his over-wrap and struggled to warm himself. She was taken aback by the traumatized look on his face, for she had never seen this side of him before. Reaching out in a hurry to help him remove a thick hide of snow-laden buffalo fur, she uncharacteristically let her arm fall across his shoulder. Grateful for the comfort of her kindness, Hans reached up and placed his rough hand over hers. "Thanks," he said, his gratitude evident in his words and the genuine smile that accompanied them. Mahal hesitated, before she pulled her hand away and tucked it safely in the protective wrap of her own blanket, holding it there while he warmed himself. "We got cattle scattered everywhere," he went on. "No tellin' how many we've already lost. It's dangerous out there—a white-out from here to town. Power line's down, drifts so high it looks like hell froze over. I barely made it."

"But you're here now," Mahal reassured him as she covered his shoulders with an Indian blanket that had been lying close to the fire and was warmed.

"Is Jon home?"

Mahal shook her head. "No, he took Fjord in the wagon with him to town this morning. I haven't seen him all day."

"Well, I hope he holed himself up somewhere. There's not much that can survive a blizzard like this one. If I wasn't more than halfway home before this hit I would have done the same."

Mahal thought about Jon and how she had helped him hitch up the wagon early that morning, dropping a handful of sugar cubes into his coat pocket for the horses. Fjord had been overly excited knowing he was set to ride along and had leapt into the driver's seat before Jon could even take hold of the reins. Of course, she was relieved that Hans had made it home, but she worried about Jon and the carefree Fjord, and prayed that they were safe.

"Did the boy make it here for chores?"

"No," said Mahal. "When the weather took a turn for the worse, I turned the horses into the barn myself. By then I knew he wasn't coming, and there was no time to waste."

Mahal watched Hans as he warmed himself by stretching his arms out toward the fire, and she felt consoled by his presence, grateful that he was only shaken, but otherwise unharmed. A great weight had been lifted from her shoulders now that she was not alone, and she felt the sense of security that a capable man like Hans exudes.

"Let me get you something hot to eat. I've been cooking stew all day, and it will help to warm you."

"Thanks. I'd really appreciate that. I haven't had a bite since breakfast near on twelve hours ago."

As Mahal turned to the cupboard to find a bowl for the stew, the memory of his touch ignited softer thoughts of him. Yes, he was gruff and plain spoken, but he moved gracefully for a man over six feet tall. And since she'd been at the house, she'd periodically seen little things that gave her the impression that there might be another side of Hans, too.

Some nights after dinner, when Jon had gone off to his study and she puttered in the kitchen, she'd hear the ancient sounds of a small bone flute that Hans played as he rested near the parlor room fire. At first she found the high, feathery tones of the flute strange, but the more she listened, the more enchanting they became, conjuring up images of dancing fairies, or "Little People" as they were called by the Ojibwa.

"What music is he playing?" she asked Jon one evening when he wandered back into the kitchen after something hot to drink.

"Viking ships sailing out to sea," he had replied. "They played those flutes on the boats way back then."

Mahal was mesmerized by the lyrical melodies and on the evenings Hans played, she lingered in the kitchen long after her work was done, enjoying the dream-like quality of the harmony that resonated deep within her. Sometimes, she sat at the small kitchen table and closed her eyes to absorb the music and imagine herself in some far off place.

One day, when both of the men were out of the house, she wandered back to Jon's study and scanned the bookshelf for one of the Viking books that she had seen him paging through. There, on the cover of one of the books was a boat unlike anything she had ever seen, with its long, graceful body, symmetrical pointed ends, the elaborately carved dragon head gracing the prow, the billowing square sail—all so magnificent. It was nothing at all like the simple birch-bark canoes with which the Ojibwa people navigated the waters. The image had stuck in her mind and thereafter whenever Hans played his flute she pictured herself on that same ship, sailing out on the lake that felt like the sea, far beyond the horizon to some mysterious land that she could only imagine.

CHAPTER ELEVEN

Mahal dished out a generous portion of the stew and turned to find Hans was still standing, bent as close to the fire as the heat would allow. She pulled over a kitchen chair, set the meal on a small table next to it and coaxed him to relax there as he ate.

When he had rested and was satiated, she broke the news of the shattered window. "There is a tree branch," she told him. "The wind blew it through the window in the parlor. It was a horrible crash. I tried to shore it up as best I could, but I'm afraid much of the cold air is still blowing in."

"I'll go take a look." Hans glanced up with genuine concern in his eyes. "It's definitely rough out there, and I guess there's nothin' can't be expected in weather like this."

Picking up the two kerosene lamps, Mahal walked with Hans back to the parlor where the wind that was easily finding every open crevice had dropped the temperature in the room at least ten degrees already. The parlor was cold and dark even with the light cast by the lanterns, but it was enough for Mahal to notice the look of surprise on Hans' face when he laid eyes on the large branch whose top limbs were splayed across the parlor room floor. Hans turned and handed his lantern to Mahal.

"My God, Mahal. When did this happen? You must have been scared out of your mind when you heard this thing come through." Hans was leaning against the body of the tree branch at the thickest part, pushing at it, testing it's weight like a man does when he's hoping to move a stubborn boulder from a field. "Damn," he grunted, glancing up. "You could have been killed if you'd been in here. I've never seen the likes of this before. I'll have to saw it off and board up the window to keep the snow out. You're not hurt?"

"I was in the kitchen when I heard the crash. I'm fine, but for a small cut on my hand that I got when I tried to stuff the blankets into the opening. I was afraid I might freeze to death if I didn't get it at least partly plugged up." She was lifting both of the lamps to better steer the light for him. "I heard this sound, like an explosion. I couldn't imagine what it could be. It was," she took a couple of steps toward him, "the most terrifying thing."

"I'm sorry you were here alone."

"I'm all right, now that you're here."

"Good," Hans said, taking one of the lanterns from her hand and holding it up to the jagged window. He swung the lantern higher to get a better look, running his hand over the area where she had forced the blankets into the opening. "I can hardly believe that you were able to get these blankets stuffed in here all by yourself and come out with only a small cut," he was saying, "It's holding, too." When he was finished packing a couple of small cracks with rags, he turned and smiled a smile that comforted her again.

The subtle compliment almost seemed unnatural coming from a man like Hans, but took it in stride. "Thank you," she said.

"I'll have to saw the thing into firewood in order to get it out. It's too heavy to move in one piece, but, it's late and I'm tired," Hans went on. "I'll have to get to it in the morning. Why don't you go back to the fire where it's warm," he suggested, the concern for her evident in his tone. "I need to check the rest of the house and change into some dry clothes. I'll be back."

CHAPTER TWELVE

"Mahal," Hans said when he returned a short while later. "I hate to leave you alone again, but if you think you'll be okay I'd like to go out and try to take care of a few things in the barn before it gets even worse out there."

Fear quickened in Mahal's gut at the thought of Hans leaving, but she knew it was not her place to question him. "I'll be okay," she replied with a confidence held thinly in her voice. "What will you do?"

"I'm going to knot a safety rope to the porch rail and walk myself to the barn," Hans said ducking his big frame into the doorway of the kitchen. "The animals have got to have food and water, and we'll need all the wood I can carry in from the porch. I'm concerned about how the temperature in the house is dropping, and I don't want to take any chances of losing this fire during the night."

"There's a good supply of wood out there," Mahal looked up from her spot close to the flames of the fire. "Jon loaded it before he left for town."

"We should be all right," Hans replied. "I'll bring in what we need for the night. I'm certain this will have all blown over by sun-up."

Mahal's eyes darted to the window where the visibility was close to zero. "Please be careful," she called after him.

Hans turned and their eyes momentarily locked as he collected the supplies, replying only, "Safety first."

Silently, Mahal watched Hans shine the lantern into the pantry. The safety rope was there, coiled up on the highest shelf and he yanked it down along with a dry sheepskin coat stuck on a wall peg, which he tossed onto the kitchen table along with a wool scarf that had been knitted by his mother. One end of the fringe had been chewed off by Fjord when he was a puppy, but other than that it was like new.

As Hans worked his arms into the heavy coat, Mahal noticed how long and thick his hair had grown since she'd first come to live there, and how Indian-like it was for him to wear it tied back like that. She took a step toward the mantle where the scent of wet wool and drying cowhide was pungent. His leather gloves had been hung there to dry, and she brushed against him in the flickering light.

It's so dark," she said, kneading the leather gloves that had stiffened. "How will you see?"

"I don't have to see," he told her, wrapping the muffler around his face and head then pulling on a fur hat. "That's what the rope is for."

When the gloves had softened up, she handed them to him. "I'm not worried that the rope should break, but, there is no light in the barn."

"There's matches and a good kerosene lantern to the left of the door once I get there. I'll be cinched and tied to the rope on the way back. If you hold a lamp to the window that will help, too."

Now more than anything, she did not want Hans to go. "Must you do this tonight? As you said, by tomorrow it will be over. I'm sure the animals can last the night, though I didn't leave them anything. I was so afraid of not making it back to the house myself."

"Cold's one thing, but hunger's another. They need fuel to survive even one night in temperatures like this. I'll be okay. I'm rested and the rope is strong. Just keep the lamp burning high, and I'll be back before you know it. I'll deal with the firewood before I head out though."

Hans spent the next hour shoveling a path to the porch wood and piling the logs up inside the door for Mahal to move to an area they had cleared along one side of the hearth. It was important to get as much wood as possible away from the drifting snow, and she laid it out to dry as best she could, knowing she would need Hans to stack it later, so that it took up less space in the already cramped room. When that was done, Hans rested and warmed himself with a mug of cider before readying himself to head back out.

Mahal was surprised at the depth of her concern as she watched Hans knot the heavy rope around his waist before looping and securing it to the porch rail. The red barn was not visible from the house, and within seconds of his venturing out, it was as if Hans had vanished into a hollow white cave. Agonizing about whether or not he had made it to the barn, she tried to busy herself, pushing the kitchen table to the window sill and settling the oil lamp up on a pile of Jon's horticulture books, praying it would blaze strong enough for him to see through the murky glass. Staring into the darkness left her even more edgy though, so she melted snow that Hans had brought in earlier in a clean kitchen bucket and washed up the plates, wiping down the table several times to ease her worrying. Opening the door even a crack was harrowing, but when all of the cleaning was done, she took the chance, fighting the wind but managing to fill every container she could find with more of the clean, white snow. When she could think of nothing else to do, she dropped into one of the stiff kitchen chairs and pulled up close to the lamp, praying that Hans, guided by the rope and the light, would soon find his way back.

But he didn't return after what seemed like an eternity, and in her helplessness Mahal turned again to the Great Spirit. *Great Spirit, you have placed a road of difficulties in our path. Shed your light and please bring us safely to the place where all good things dwell.*

Exhausted by the stress of the day, Mahal wanted more than anything to close her eyes and rest, but she was so worried about Hans that all she could do was sit at the hard square table and cradle her head in her arms. Drifting back to happier times when she was so small she couldn't ride by herself, she remembered how her mother would tie her to the saddle so that she wouldn't slip off, and they'd ride for hours through open fields and winding trails, stopping now and then to let the horse chew on the grass or drink from a shady stream. Imagining her mother's arms around her and the power of the horse below, for a moment Mahal felt safe. It seemed as if the Great Spirit was doing his job.

CHAPTER THIRTEEN

Touched by the caring that Mahal had so clearly expressed and impressed that she had taken it upon herself to deal as best she could with the shattered window, Hans found himself thinking about her strength of spirit as he bedded down the animals, breaking out extra bales of hay from the loft and strapping every blanket he could find around the horses. Then, he shoved back the barn door enough to fill a tin basin with snow and melted it over a fire he had built in another steel tub. As the horses drank their fill, Hans poured extra water into a trough and warmed a pan of milk for his beloved cats. He left out every scrap of food in the rain barrel as well as another bag of beef jerky that he found in his saddlebag.

When he had done all that he could do, he knotted himself again to the rope and began to pull himself hand-over-fist back to the house. The snow grew deeper as he trudged on, the worst thing being the swirling ice-crystals that blasted his half-exposed face, so razor-sharp and blinding that he had to drop his head to his chest and close his eyes. The snow that drifted almost up to his knees made it difficult to walk a straight line, and the cold was so bitter and the wind so strong that twice he was thrown off balance. Hans was shocked at how hard he had to struggle to get back on his feet, but he forced himself to keep moving until finally he caught a glimpse of the lamplight glowing in the window. Minutes later, in one final push to the end, he thrust himself onto the porch.

"Hans!" Mahal cried out, jolted from her daydream by the commotion outside. She jumped up and flung open the door.

"Get back," Hans shouted, a gust of wind spraying her with snow. "Stay inside."

After several agonizing minutes, he pushed open the door and tumbled in. "Hans!" Mahal tugged at the rope knot to free him, pulling off his frozen coat and gloves and the thick wool sweater beneath. "I was so worried! Come closer to the fire and let me help you get warm." Hans' flannel shirt and long cotton undershirt were soaked to the skin, and he looked as if he'd been in a rainstorm rather than a blizzard.

"It's okay," he gasped. "I'm good now that I'm here."

This time, Hans shivered near the fire in silence, yanking off his boots and peeling off layers of wet clothes. Mahal kept busy snatching them up off the floor, and when she glanced back at him, he was stripped to the waist with his shoulders hunched toward the flames.

Mahal had kept a blanket for him warming by the fire, and she reached for it now and laid it over his shoulders.

I should have warmed a dozen blankets for him instead of daydreaming, she admonished herself. The well-defined muscles in Hans' back flexed as he drew the blanket over himself, and when he turned his head to move closer to the warmth, she caught the profile of his face—the strong, square jaw, the long straight nose. She could see that his lips were still quivering. *I should have had a hot drink waiting. Instead the fire is low,* she chided herself again, hurrying to add a log of wood to the fire.

Hans reached out and touched a hand to her shoulder. "Thank you for warming the blanket," he said. "I'm going back for some dry clothes. I won't be long."

Mahal clanged around for a pan to heat the cider, and by the time it had grown hot on the cook top, Hans was back fumbling with the buttons on his shirt.

"I hate to say it, but it's as bad as I've ever seen it," he said reaching for a mug of the hot cider Mahal held out to him. Clearly Hans was concerned, but when he saw the worried look on Mahal's face, he hastily added: "It can't last forever though. I can't imagine it won't have blown itself out by morning."

Of course Mahal wanted to believe him, but native instincts about weather wouldn't allow her to completely let her guard down.

"See, it's quieting down," he said. "Listen." Every now and then the wind did indeed soften to a lesser howl, and Hans began to point out lulls in an attempt to ease her mind.

As safe as Mahal felt with Hans, being alone with him like this ignited confusion and attraction of equal proportions. Before tonight, Mahal had only known Hans to ignore her. He'd rarely even spoken to her since her arrival in Gustafson Corridor. On occasion he would be late arriving home after she and Jon had eaten and their plates had been washed. She went out of her way to avoid him if she could, rushing up the narrow stairs to her room when she heard his horse trotting into the farmyard. Peeking out the window, her eyes watched as he trudged from the barn to the house. She would return to the kitchen only when she knew he had finished washing up and had gone off to the dining room to wait for his food. Sometimes he checked with her to see if Jon was in his study, but mostly he waited patiently at the dining room table, knowing that she had heard him come in. Their eyes rarely met when she served him, not even a comment about the food, good or bad. There were times when it was so uncomfortable, that if it hadn't been for Jon's presence in the house, she thought she never would have lasted a week. But tonight was different. The man that was with her now did not seem like the man that she had gone out of her way to avoid, and Mahal was more than grateful for Hans' company as the wind and ice, like tribal drums, continued to beat a relentless rhythm down upon the house.

Side-by-side, Mahal and Hans worked to bring some order to the wood pile along the kitchen wall, and when they had finished, the sight of the rustic logs stacked floor to ceiling gave them a sense of satisfaction and safety. It was clear there was enough to last them for a couple of days if they were careful, but Hans doubted that would be necessary.

"I'm going to light the bedroom fires," he said, lugging an armful of wood up the tight staircase, first to Mahal's room and then back down to the old master bedroom at the far side of the house where he now slept.

When he returned to the kitchen, Mahal was waiting with a couple of warmed extra blankets folded for them to take back to their respective rooms.

The truth was, Mahal didn't want to leave the warmth of the kitchen or the comfort of Hans' company, but she didn't want to let on that she still harbored a good amount of fear as to what the night would bring. And so she said nothing and took a step toward the staircase to retire to her room.

As if he could read her mind, Hans looked up and caught her eye. "We'll be all right," he said. "We've got plenty of wood inside now, and I'm sure all of this will have blown out by sun-up and someone will be along to help us dig out. Ease yourself. Go and get a good night's rest."

Chapter Fourteen

In the deep hours of the night, however, the temperature sank to a bone-chilling low, and the wind sang a never-ending song of fury as all three fires burned dangerously close to embers. The drastic shift in the temperature woke Mahal out of a fitful sleep, and she wandered downstairs layered in blankets and fur. She found Hans already in the kitchen with the Indian blanket she had given him earlier draped over his shoulders, rifling through the wood pile, cherry picking the driest logs to rekindle the fire to a more comfortable level. The scent of the low burning logs was heavy in the air, and Mahal coughed as she waved away a stream of smoke, clearing her eyes and quickly sizing up the situation.

"I was just about to wake you" said Hans. "I guess you heard me shuffling around."

"The cold woke me," Mahal answered, grabbing a handful of birch bark from the tinder box and tossing it into the smoldering fire just as Hans was laying on the first dry log. In a second the flames took hold, and she moved back while he set in two more of the largest and driest logs, then re-lit the stove.

With the fire stoked, Hans felt around the window where the bulky frame did not fit snuggly into the wall and where a steady stream of the outside air was seeping into the room. He worked steadily, folding two blankets so that they were plenty thick and then nailing them over the window to minimize the draft. When he was done, he turned toward Mahal who was huddled by the fire while she watched him work.

"Yes, I agree," he said, acknowledging her posture, "It's best we stay right here and hunker near the fire and stove. I'm going to pull those two oversized chairs in from the parlor. We'll be more comfortable that way."

To make room for the chairs, Hans dragged the eating table away from the window and shoved it into a corner. He opened the door and stepped into the dining room, which was chilly enough, but when he went into the parlor for the chairs, he was slapped with a blast of frigid outside air proving that the blankets and rags Mahal and he had fashioned to plug the broken window were no match for the powerful storm. Hans knew that no matter what, he would somehow have to get the tree branch out of the room come the first sign of morning and shore up the busted opening. Wasting no time, Hans dragged the chairs, one by one, back into the kitchen, drawing them as close to the hearth as was safe. Here he and Mahal could curl up in them and use the fire as well as the stove to warm themselves.

"I think you should find your warmest wrappings and bring them down here," Hans said to Mahal. "I'm going to close off the doors to all of the rooms and plug the drafts so we can harness as much heat in here as possible."

Mahal made her way up the narrow kitchen stairs, collecting quilts and pillows off the beds in the empty rooms including the buffalo wrap Elias had given her on her first ride in with Jon that she kept draped over the foot of her bed. With her arms full, she ventured back into the kitchen where Hans was already nailing two planks of wood crisscross over the kitchen window that was clattering loudly under the blankets against what sounded like tornado force winds.

"This will help keep the glass from blowing out tonight," he said, when Mahal's troubled eyes briefly met his. "I guess I didn't realize until now that we had a weak window in here."

Mahal knew that it was the ferocity of the storm, not the weakness of the window that was causing him to take this precaution, but she appreciated the concern expressed for her by the lie.

When the work was done, Hans splashed hearty pours of Scotch into two glasses and offered one to Mahal. "No, thank you," she said at first, but he continued to hold it toward her, assuring her it would help keep her warm from the inside out. To her surprise, she relaxed as she slowly sipped and allowed the heat of the liquor to seep into her body, warming her just as he'd promised. It wasn't long before she dozed off, cocooned on one of the big chairs under blankets and skins with her legs curled up comfortably beneath her.

As tired as Hans was, the effect of the drink could not counterbalance the angst he was feeling about the ferocity of the storm and their limited supply of firewood. He was kicking himself for not bringing more of the wood inside and sat wide-awake in the chair next to Mahal with the kind of restlessness that extremes of stress and exhaustion bring. He couldn't remember when he'd ever felt this weary. He stared into the fire, mesmerized by its brilliance, keeping quiet so as not to disturb Mahal. As the wind and snow pummeled the house, he rested his eyes, listening and wrestling with the uneasy feeling that had lodged itself deep in his gut. The weather seemed determined to show them no mercy, and he listened for any aberrations in the noise outside that at times was as deafening as a runaway train. Mahal, he knew, was sleeping fitfully, dreaming dreams clearly stoked by fear. Hans studied her face in the amber glow, and after awhile, when she cried out, he leaned his large frame forward and put a hand to her shoulder.

"Mahal, wake up," he said, gently prodding her shoulder to rouse her. "You're having a bad dream."

Mahal stirred and blinked her eyes, taking a minute to orient herself. In spite of the cold, she had drifted into a deep sleep, dreaming that she was tramping through a lonely forest with the shadow of Windigo at her back waiting to pounce.

"Come here," Hans whispered. The fire had found it's center and shadows bounced gently off the walls. "Sit next to me. I'm gonna' have to let this fire burn down a bit to preserve the wood and this chair's plenty big for both of us. There's no use freezing to death. We can keep each other warm."

Even keeping the fire at a medium burn they could easily go through twenty logs a night, he figured, a luxury he was beginning to doubt they had. As the night progressed and the storm intensified, Hans had to admit to himself that he might have been too optimistic about its duration. From here on out, he had to do his best to conserve what wood they had. When Mahal did not move, Hans tried again. Finally, he pulled himself up and reached his arm out to her. "Don't worry. I'm not talking about anything more than sharing body heat," he said. "It's okay."

Mahal hesitated, still feeling unsure as to why this man, who had only spoken his first kind word to her a few hours earlier, would be reaching for her now. Her body shuddered. And then, as if it had been cued for an orchestra, the wind snapped a chord that rattled every window in the house with such ferocity that Mahal, in a moment of uncharacteristic trust, reached for Hans' hand and tucked herself in next to him.

Hans folded her into his arms, barely touching his chin to her head, catching a whiff of the baking sugar caught up in her hair. Cradled against his body, Mahal let her eyes slide shut, surprised at how safe she felt in his arms, deeply grateful to not be alone on such a dangerous night. He smelled clean like the cold air and the soap she'd come to know in the house, scents that were familiar by now and made her feel at home. Warmed by the heat of his body, she began to relax. Lying there against him, Mahal could feel the muscles of his chest, the rise and fall of his steady breathing, the strength in the arms that looped around her. Being close to him helped to drown out the noise of the storm, as well, and she felt comforted listening to the pop and crackle of the fire, aware of their breathing, soft and rhythmic. Pressing her ear gently to his heart, she found the steady beat quieted her fears and soothed her like a warm rub of oil. As she rested, Hans maneuvered the buffalo blanket, wrapping them in tighter, closer, deeper, and they slept like this, locked together with only the darkness to gauge the time. Sometime in the latest hours of the night, Hans awakened and became aware that the comfort of their hold had somehow become an embrace. Mahal was clearly secure with him now, and he with her.

In time, Mahal shifted to adjust herself, tilting her head up to see if she had stirred Hans. In an instant, her eyes met his, and when she tasted the subtle smoothness of the Scotch that lingered on his lips, she returned his kiss with an abandon and trust she had never felt with anyone before. Hans stood up then, cradling her in his arms, allowing the hefty buffalo hide to fall to the floor. Nudging it closer to the fire with his foot, he laid Mahal gently down on top of it before drawing an armful of blankets and quilts off the chairs to cover them. In time they came together in the dark spaces of the night and the yellow light of the fire, oblivious to the implications of what was happening, aware only that it was powerful, and that it was good.

For Mahal, their lovemaking was like nothing she had ever known. Hans was like a graceful warrior, gently moving her to his liking as she yielded to his touch again and again, as if she could not get enough of him. Before the storm, she had been wary of him, almost frightened at times, always feeling his disapproval of her presence in the house and of her friendship with Jon, but here in the darkness she whispered his name over and over, "Hans," she said, "Hans . . . I . . . ."

"It's okay, it's okay," he answered, "I'm right here. I've got you. You're safe now."

And so she let herself go and let him take her to places she never could have imagined. Mahal moved her hands over his great chest, and down the muscles on his arms pulling herself into him, all of her inhibitions melting away as they gave themselves to one another completely. As their breathing slowed and their bodies relaxed, Hans stroked her hair, kissing her lips, her breasts, the soft mound of her belly as he shifted the coverings, pulling them high up over their heads before they dozed off into a deep, tranquil sleep.

Hours later when they awakened, Hans grew very quiet, and Mahal sensed that he had something more to say.

"What is it?' she said as she lay in his arms. "Tell me."

"It isn't right," he told her. "I mean, I know how you feel about Jon and . . ."

"No," she stopped him. "I care about Jon, but I don't love him . . . not in this way."

"Even so," said Hans. "I'm sure he's in love with you. I've seen the way he lights up when you walk into a room, the way his eyes follow your every move. A man would have to be blind not to notice."

"If that is true," she said, "you are only seeing one side. I couldn't be with you now if I were in love with Jon or any other man."

And, having lost all sense of time, he pulled her to him once again and somewhere in the arching spaces of their bodies Hans knew that he finally understood the words of his dying Pa: that love is more important than anything.

Afterwards, Mahal slept in Hans's arms while he watched her dreaming, and when she opened her eyes, the look on her face told Hans that she too never wanted this to end. He pulled her close, both aware that words could never say what their bodies had already expressed.

CHAPTER FIFTEEN

"Are you hungry?" Hans asked Mahal hours later as they lay under the blankets and skins with only the fire for light. "I'm starving."

"Yes, me too," Mahal answered, and she looked into his eyes and knew that she had given him her heart as much as anything. *I will always want him*, she thought.

Hans slid out from under the covers, shielding himself with a blanket, and Mahal turned her head as he dressed, feeling shy over the intimacy that had come upon them so quickly. As she dressed, Hans reached for the hammer and pulled down the strips of wood and blankets from the window to see what the storm had wrought during the night, and they found themselves face-to-face with a wall of solid white.

"Are we buried in here?" asked Mahal, in a timid voice. There were feelings to sort out after what had happened between them during the night, and she was glad that his back was turned away, so that she didn't have to meet his eyes. She felt the weakness in her knees as she busied herself lighting the wood stove and filling the coffee pot with water. *What have I done?* she thought.

Hans moved away from the window and took his time jiggling the frozen kitchen doorknob. "I'd say we are definitely snowed in," he said when he finally opened it a crack and found himself confronted with a high drift of snow. "As far as I can tell from the howlin' that's still whipping up the chimney, the storm's not over yet. Stay here, by the fire. I'm going to check the rest of the rooms."

Mahal poured herself a cup of hot coffee while she waited, slowly stirring in a spoonful of sugar. The room was toasty now in spite of the conditions outside and she could make good use of the food on hand: a dozen eggs, deer sausage, and bread. She might even bake a fresh loaf of bread later if she decided to get ambitious. There were plenty of staples in the pantry and thankfully the root cellar was well stocked with meats, canned vegetables and fruit, crocks of pickles, and even a large barrel of apples that the brothers had loaded up that fall.

"Damn, it's cold," said Hans after he had made his way through the house and back to the kitchen where he was careful to reseal the bottom of the door leading to the dining room with a rolled blanket. The fire was hot enough to warm the room sufficiently after Hans had stoked it, but afterwards they kept it fueled just enough to keep it burning one precious log at a time. "I'm not sure how long we'll need to make this firewood last. Now that the room is heated up we're better off with a low, steady burn and," he paused, "body heat." He smiled warmly then, and she felt a rush of blood to her cheeks at this first reference to last night.

"We can make do," she said, smiling shyly.

If Hans was at all uncomfortable with the passion that had unfolded the previous night, he didn't show it as he busied himself rummaging a small saw out of the pantry. Luckily there were two decent sized planks of shelving wood hiding there, too, that he could use to board up the broken window once he got the tree branch out. Wasting no time, he turned to attend to business in the parlor room where a heavy draft still threatened their efforts to stay warm. The project took longer than Mahal had expected, but when she heard him hammering an oilcloth over the compromised wall, she knew that he had nearly finished.

Hans proceeded to give her a more detailed report of their situation as he returned the saw to its spot in the pantry. "Storm's still raging, but the good news is that the backside of the house is not completely snowed over, and the upstairs windows are frosty but otherwise clear. The only thing I could make out was a blur of the tree line way off in the distance, but I'm pretty sure the house must be visible, at least on the backside. When this storm ends, it might be best to start digging out from one of the lower bedrooms on that side of the house."

"I thought it would be over by now. I've never seen a blizzard last this long," said Mahal.

"That makes two of us," Hans agreed. "But we both know how unpredictable the weather is out here. Storms can be as stubborn as people sometimes." He was absorbed in slicing several more pieces of the sausage before laying it back down on the plate. "One thing for sure," he said between bites, "it can't last forever."

"At least we have food," said Mahal, making a weak attempt to be upbeat as she watched him turn his attention to the dwindling stack of wood, feeding the largest and driest logs into the fire. "He is so capable," she thought, "I wish I could tell him that I don't know what I would have done if he hadn't made it through . . . How much I love . . ."

"I'm more worried about running out of wood," Hans said, interrupting her thoughts. "I know there's wood piled on the porch, but it'll take hours to dig it out from under the drifts, and it will have to dry out before it's usable anyway. We can last for a couple of days, but after that, blizzard or not, I'll have to somehow get to it." When Hans saw the fear in Mahal's eyes, he stepped over and curled an arm around her. "Listen to me," he said, pulling her in close against his body. "You don't have to worry about anything. I'll protect you no matter what. You hear me? Let me help you cook us up a nice breakfast with whatever we've got, and we'll wait it out. I'm starving, and you must be, too."

There was a pause for a sudden whip of the wind in the chimney, a squeeze of Hans' arm over her shoulders, and then Mahal said bravely, "I'm good now, and yes, I'm hungry, too. Let me see about getting our breakfast together."

Hans cut slices of bread while Mahal slid a square of butter into the pan and scrambled up the eggs with the rest of the sausage, then browned the thick slices of bread in the skillet. When they had eaten their fill, they spent the morning together huddled near the fire, bundled under the blankets and skins, sharing stories of their upbringing, carefully avoiding talk of how both of their worlds had been jolted and their private musings about what lay ahead as a result.

Around noon, Hans went upstairs to check the sunlight in the bedroom windows that were frosted but clear enough to become a primitive gauge of time according to the amount of light they let in. On his way back downstairs he tugged an old photo album from a shelf in Jon's study and slipped it on the seat of one of the table chairs to show to Mahal later. Mahal glanced over her shoulder at him when he re-entered the room.

"Can you tell what time it is?" she asked him.

"Only that it's daylight. I'd guess early afternoon, but the storm hides the sunlight, so that I can't even tell where it is in the sky. I can't believe I forgot to wind the clocks," he grinned. "Guess I was just focused on something . . . or someone else."

Mahal smiled and snapped the flour tin closed. "Are you hungry? The bread needs to cook a bit," she said, "but I can begin to prepare something now."

"Always, hungry!" Hans answered, "but what do we have? Maybe I should go down into the cellar and see what's there."

"Yes, please" she said. "I'm afraid the stew is gone, and we've no fresh vegetables or meat up here at all."

Mahal watched as Hans made his way down into the root cellar for a large, cured ham that he was certain was there, and later, when the loaf of bread came out of the oven, they shared the warm slices slathered in butter with the salty meat. The snow and wind continued to beat down upon the house, but the refuge they had discovered in each other hibernating there in the small, walled-off kitchen had mitigated their fears of the fury and cold and made them grateful for the blizzard that had brought them together. They ate in front of the fireplace hearth, and after their meal, Hans helped her carry their dishes to the sink where she washed them in water they got from melting snow.

Mahal was about to curl back up near the fire when she noticed the photo album on the seat of one of the kitchen chairs. When Hans saw it in her hand he looked up.

"Oh, I dug that out this afternoon. Here, sit down," he said indicating the buffalo wrap on the floor where they'd spent the night. "I want to show you something." He sat down next to her and opened the album, holding it up between them.

"I wanted to show you my family members I was talking about this morning. These are my parents at Ellis Island," he began, pointing to a fuzzy photograph of his father and mother, two shabby, worn-out suitcases between them, alongside two adolescent boys who appeared dazed, staring at the camera from inside what must have been the immigrant processing center in New York. "That's Bjorn and Emil," Hans said, eager to explain the photos that, though black and white, clearly captured the squalor and uncertainty on the faces of the subjects.

"You must have been so frightened to have been left like that," said Mahal, sitting up taller so that she could better view the images. She understood how much these photographs meant to Hans. Photographs of any kind were a luxury that only money or happenstance provided. She thought now of the one small sepia-toned photograph of her father that her mother had given her, the only image of him that she held in her memory. All she could make out was his face, stoic and unsmiling under a large coonskin hat, planted on the banks of a stream with a beaver trap at his feet and a shotgun in his hand, looking every bit the frontiersman that people said he was. How many nights had she made up stories about him as she held up to candlelight the expressionless face staring back at her?

"Worst day of my life," said Hans. "Watching that ship pull away was terrifying. I didn't know if I would ever see them again. The only good thing was Jon was too young to remember. They didn't even bring him to the dock to wave goodbye, and it's something I'll never forget."

"At least you have a family," said Mahal, the wistfulness in her voice not lost to this newly attentive Hans.

"What about you?" he asked. "I know about your family, but what about your husband?" The word "husband" hung in the air between them like a cumbersome weight. For the first time Hans felt uncomfortable and was sorry that he'd even mentioned him.

"Well," Mahal answered reluctantly. "I thought I loved my husband in the beginning, but he is an angry man, and now, since his accident, he's even worse. There are times when he comes at me and my mother-in-law tries to stop him. She's a kind woman and has been like a mother to me since my own mother died. Sometimes he listens to her, but not always. It has been difficult."

Hans remembered hearing some vague reference to an unfit husband, but he hadn't paid it much attention. Now he wanted to hear more. "I'm sorry," he said. "You deserve someone who treats you right." But when she did not elaborate, he turned the page of the photograph album and continued.

"Hey, I recognize that," she pointed to the knife in the portrait of Hans' father as a young man back in Norway. The antler-horn knife, its blade encased in a leather sheath, was fastened to a belt around his waist and was clearly visible in the grainy photograph.

"Yes, it belonged to my father," Hans explained to her. "I can still hear his voice low in my ear, 'Take this, son,' he said to me when we were standing on the dock and they were about to board the ship. He told me he loved me and to watch over Jon and that as soon as he could he would send money for our fare. That was the last I saw of any of them until seven long years later. I've treasured that knife all my life."

"That's sad and beautiful," said Mahal. "I only knew my mother, though she always pointed out that I have my father's eyes."

"Did you not know him at all?"

"No, I only have the photograph that's upstairs in my room and the stories that I make up from looking at the picture. I know that he held me in his arms and gave me my name, which is not in the Ojibwa custom. Sometimes I think about it, you know, the same way you think about a dream that fades over time but never loses its power."

"I know how painful it is growing up without a father," said Hans. "Every couple of months we'd get a letter, and I remember pouring over them. Between Jon and myself, the paper was worn thin. But your life has been even harder. You've had little support, and you've lived with an abusive husband." He rose and walked to the door. Unfastening the knife and sheath from his belt that hung on the peg rack near the door, Hans returned to Mahal and looked directly into her eyes. "I want you to take this," he said, pressing the knife into her hand. "If he ever tries to hurt you again, I want you to use it to protect yourself."

"No, I can't take something like that," she said, her tone growing more subdued. "I've managed this long. This is a keepsake from your father and as such it is sacred. You must not give it away."

"I want you to have it, Mahal. Take it, please," he insisted, placing the knife in her hand and closing his hand over hers. "It will make me happy to know that you have something to defend yourself with if you need to."

For a few moments Mahal stared at the knife, then she slid it out of its sheath and ran her fingers over the oiled stag handle admiring its beauty and the way it attached to the blade, so polished it almost looked brand new. She put her head down and said a silent prayer, taking the meaning of this gift into her heart, then she looked up at Hans and her eyes met his. "Thank you," she said, "I will treasure this as you have."

Hans was mesmerized by her heart-felt gratitude and the light in her jeweled eyes. He reached for her face, touching it lightly, and he was again overwhelmed by the rush of sensuality that had ignited his senses last night. He kissed her deeply and drew her to him, and once again their inhibitions melted and the passion they had tucked away since they'd awakened hours ago overtook them. They surrendered again to each other and to the purity of the moment.

CHAPTER SIXTEEN

Hans and Mahal made love off and on as the hours drifted by, and they grew more and more content with each other. When they weren't in each other's arms, they found small projects to do, Mahal mending a basket, Hans cleaning his rifle, polishing his knives, and tending to the ever-needy fire. Eventually though, the chill in the air got the better of Mahal, and she set her project aside and returned to the blankets and chair. There she allowed herself to bask in the warmth of the fire and this new found love, so unlike any that had come before. When thoughts of her husband snuck in and threatened to ruin her reverie, she banished them to a dark corner of her mind where she chose to shine no light. Later, she sliced the remainder of the bread, and they ate what was left of the ham, along with a round of cow's cheese that Hans had retrieved from the cellar.

"Would you play your flute for me?" she asked him when the dishes were done, and she was wrapped up and comfortable again by the fire.

Pleased by her request, Hans took up the instrument and began to play. Mahal snuggled deeper into the chair, indulging the daydreams sparked by the romantic nature of the music. She imagined she was with Hans on a Viking ship, and they were sailing out on the great lake on a beautiful summer day as the music became the breeze that filled their sails.

Mahal was dozing on and off lingering in her daydream when Hans laid down his flute and slipped away to check the light in the upstairs window. When he returned, he told her that the sky was dark and that nighttime had come. "The wind has died down though," he said. "There is a big difference from what it's been these last couple of days. I think the storm's finally blowing itself out. We could be looking at a clear sky come morning." As he spoke their eyes met and they silently made love again in the warmth of the fire. Mahal felt the power of Han's body as he moved above her, all muscle and grace, taking her and once again claiming her as his own. She had never been so physically fulfilled, as she surrendered to the magic of their lovemaking again and again.

A time was coming though, when the sun would shine, Jon would arrive, they'd dig themselves out, and life would return to the way it had been before nature and fate had thrown them together. Neither one of them wanted to imagine what it would be like for them when that time came. "Mahal," Hans spoke her name gently, with great care. "We have to talk about what's going to happen when the weather clears up and Jon returns."

"I know," she said, resignation and sadness defining both her tone and the look in her eyes as she gazed into the fire.

"Mahal," he tried again, "if you want to, we can work something out. I can talk to Jon, explain to him what's happened here and how we feel about each other. Maybe he'll understand. But if you have feelings for him, please tell me now."

Mahal stood up and drifted over to the sink, leaning her hands on the porcelain edge as she struggled with her thoughts and emotions. She squeezed her eyes shut to keep herself from crying, but her back was turned, and Hans couldn't tell what she was thinking or what she was feeling.

"Say something," he finally said. "It's important. Do you love me as much as I love you?"

As he waited for her reply, Hans was overcome with fear of losing her. No woman had ever felt better to him than Mahal. Making love to her, holding her in his arms, watching her sleep felt right . . . he had never been so captured by a woman. Liaisons with women in town were empty and had never meant anything. The absence of love that had kept him in an emotional vacuum for so long had vanished in the short time he'd been with Mahal, and there was no turning back. But still he worried about the magnitude of it all and what it meant. He hung his head in the silence and waited.

She finally spoke up. "It's not Jon," she said, almost in a whisper, turning her body to face him. "I care deeply about him, and I will be forever grateful to him for being so kind and bringing me here, but as I've told you, I could never feel for him what I have come to feel for you these past days. My marriage was arranged, and I realize now that when I married my husband, I didn't know what love was. In the early years he had moments of kindness, and I tried to convince myself that I loved him, but I never could and over time he became more and more controlling and obsessive. Now, since the accident, he has fits of anger that are as violent and terrifying as they are unpredictable, but, I am an Ojibwa woman. I am married within the laws of my people, and there are obligations that go along with marriage vows that extend far beyond the promise I made to my husband."

"But you can change that, Mahal. Ojibwa do get divorced."

"Yes, I know it is permitted, but it would cause a lot of upset and bring shame to my mother-in-law who has been so good to me. She is an old woman and has not had an easy life. It would break her heart."

"I can't imagine life without you in it." Hans was earnest. "I'll build us a house up north away from Gustafson Corridor if you want. We can work things out. Will you at least think about it?"

CHAPTER SEVENTEEN

It was the quiet that woke them on the morning of the third day. They'd gotten so used to the constant din of the storm that when they realized it was gone, they looked at each other silently, then rushed to dress. When Hans peered out of the upstairs bedroom window his eyes feasted on a patch of clear, blue sky. Just as he had suspected, the great blizzard was finally over.

"Mahal," he shouted, his boots sounding down the tight kitchen staircase as he hurried to tell her the news. "The storm is done. Most likely someone will find us by nightfall."

"Yes," she said. "Jon will return home as soon as he can, I expect." Suddenly it seemed like there was so much to do. Beneath the growing anticipation that help was on the way were unsettling layers of ambiguity and fear. Their imminent rescue was so monumental that it overshadowed everything, including their unresolved relationship, and they rushed around in an effort to tidy up the house and not betray what had taken place within its walls.

The morning light had broken clear over the snow-choked fields hours ago, but Hans and Mahal could see nothing over the heavy white mass that had drifted up over the ground floor windows on the front side of the house, blocking their view. But though the house was mostly buried on that side, the chimneys and stovepipe still rose up like pillars from some ancient world, providing a visible landmark for Jon or anyone approaching the site. Out back, the snow banks had piled unevenly, leaving some of the windows only partially blocked. When they looked out, it was nothing more than a sea of white.

After an early lunch, Mahal and Hans returned to each other once more in the warmth of the fire, their love making now fueled by an urgency neither one was willing to give voice to. Hans wanted to experience all of her—to know and embrace all that was behind those hauntingly beautiful eyes. He wanted to know her like no one else who had come before him knew her, and he drew her to himself once again and entered her body with a passion he'd never known he had.

Dozing in the sweetness of their lovemaking, they were startled awake by a clambering that seemed to be coming from the backside of the house. When the faint echo of a dog's bark signaled the identity of the *rescuers*, Hans and Mahal's eyes met, and they embraced one another with an intensity that spoke volumes.

As the sounds intensified, Hans and Mahal quickly dressed and started toward the back bedroom down the hall from Jon's study. They could hear Fjord's bark clearly now, and Mahal's heart quickened with nervous apprehension at the thought of seeing Jon after all that had happened. With the sound of the barking dog so close, she knew that Jon could not be far behind.

"Hellooooo!" Someone was yelling. "Hellooooo!"

In an instant Hans realized that the greeting was coming from just outside the bedroom window.

"Hans, are you there?" Jon called out, the concern in his voice coming through loud and clear. "Mahal too?"

"Yes! We're both here!"

Jon and Elias had arrived on Indian snowshoes, pulling a sled of food supplies from town including a freshly killed rabbit that Elias had shot on the way, as well as a couple of shovels they'd thrown in at the last minute in anticipation of what they might find. Fjord was barking wildly now, perched on top of the loaded-down sled. Jon and Elias had shoveled their way in to the most accessible window, heaping white mounds of snow off to the sides. After several yards, they reached their destination where Hans and Mahal were now waiting. Hans jiggled open the window and leaned out and opened his arms to his brother. "Thank God you got here safely," he said. "We're so glad to see you." Hans offered his hand through the window opening and pulled them in one after the other.

"Glad to see you too, brother. I figured you were probably holed up in one of the camps. I was worried sick at the thought of Mahal being here alone. I sure am happy to see your faces."

"Mahal said you'd gone to town, and I knew chances were good you were at the Spauding, but still, one never knows in weather like this."

"Not as afraid as I was for you and Mahal," Jon laughed as he passed sixty pounds of restless dog through the window.

Fjord was wild to see Mahal and squirmed out of Hans' arms nearly knocking her over with excitement.

"Damn, I've never seen the likes of a storm as bad as this . . . ever!" said Jon, brushing the snow off his coat and searching Mahal's face for a spark of recognition. After fretting about her over the past few days, seeing her again was like seeing her anew, and he realized how much he'd missed her. "I was worried sick about you," he said, regarding her directly, but she only smiled shyly and cast her head down focusing her attention on Fjord. The dog was beside himself jumping and whimpering after Mahal, eliciting a happy look on her face, reminding Jon again of that first day and the jealousy he felt when Fjord got the smile he'd been craving. Then, out of the corner of his eye, Jon caught a stolen, almost furtive, look between Hans and Mahal that made his heart drop. As he watched her move about, lavishing all of her attention on Fjord and raising her eyes with interest only when the supplies were passed through the window, Jon thought that the gains he'd made with her might have blown away with the storm, and that he'd have to draw Mahal out of herself all over again. It was as if the last few of months they'd spent living under the same roof never happened—as if they'd never decorated the Christmas tree or ridden up Spirit Mountain or sat in the kitchen over cups of hot cider.

With Fjord at her heels, Mahal was the first to head back to the kitchen with an arm full of food items, including the rabbit that she intended to skin and cook that night. The others soon followed, overflowing the table and chairs with supplies, several plump chickens, fruit cocktail cups from the hotel, a jar of salted almonds, and myriad items to restock the pantry. As Mahal sorted out the treasures, the men stripped off their layers of outerwear and pressed close to the meager fire.

"What are you doin' out here, Elias?" Hans asked, sitting on the edge of the hearth. "I thought you never left the woods."

"I was in town when the storm swooped in out of nowhere. One minute it was quiet as night, the next we got snow and ice hammerin' down so bad we can't see two feet ahead of us." Elias sat up straight in one of the oversized chairs smiling at Mahal as he accepted a cup of hot coffee. "I knew my wife and kids were safe in the camp, but I couldn't have gotten home even if they wasn't, so I holed up with Jon at the Spaulding. It's a good thing I was still in town and not on the road home, or I might not 'a made it. But, I'm glad I'm here to help. I'm waiting with two other men for a wagon sled to be fixed so we can try and scrounge up some supplies before we head back to the camp in a day or so."

"There's horses and some stock in the barn," said Hans yanking his gloves off the mantle above him and twisting them to soften up the leather. He was anxious to get out of the house and take in the open sky. "Been almost three days without feed. We got to dig'em out."

"Let's get to it," said Jon distractedly, hoping to catch Mahal with his eye as she set a serving plate of hard boiled eggs, cold salami, and a loaf of bread on the hearth where the men could easily reach it. He still couldn't get a read on her, but he'd seen enough to know that she was back inside her shell and not really present—at least not for him. It was frustrating, but Jon resigned himself and turned his attention to the matters at hand.

"This is the first day anyone's dared to open a door," Jon said. "On the way out here we ran into Otto Kleve. He said others are out checking their farms, checking on neighbors—seeing who's in trouble, who needs help. The cattle will come later. We'll know the damage soon enough."

"Some is wiped out for sure," said Elias, pulling pieces of the meat from the plate and piling them, open-face on a slice of buttered bread. "You can bet on that. A man could live forever and never see the likes 'a this."

"Yeah," said Hans, "That first night, I roped myself from the house to the barn and almost didn't make it back to the house. The ice dust was so thick I could barely breath. It's deceiving."

"What'd you do cooped up here for three days?" Elias chuckled and made small talk to change the subject as he helped himself to more of the meat and bread. "Heck, here we are eatin' and you probably just want to get reoriented with the world, go on out and tilt your faces to the sky."

"It was like another world." Hans agreed. "We lost track of time that's for sure. Lost track of everything . . ."

Hans began to bundle up, and Jon and Elias hurried to swallow their last bites and follow suit.

"Wait," said Mahal. "I want to go, too."

Delighted that she was going to join them, Jon's spirits began to rise, and as she reached up to take her cloak from the wall hook, he rushed in to help, brushing against her arm and fumbling hanging items of clothing to the floor. "Oh, I'm sorry," he reddened, picking her cloak up off the floor and handing it off to her with a nervous turn. His pulse raced as it always did whenever happenstance brought her close, but there was no indication from Mahal that she even knew he was nearby. When they were ready, the four of them made their way down the hallway to the back bedroom and, one by one, strapped on snowshoes and pulled themselves through the window and into the light of day. The sun was at its highest and burning strong.

Hans and Mahal squinted in the brightness like bears coming out of hibernation. The sun glared off the snow making the light painful to the eye. Mahal dropped her eyelids then and let her head fall back. The heat of the sun beat down upon her face, and she breathed deeply, relishing the fine, clean air as Jon, Elias, and Hans picked up shovels and readied for work.

Mahal was the first to speak. "When can we get to the horses?"

"First thing," said Hans, raising up one of the shovels Jon and Elias had brought with them on the sled and trudging out onto the snow around the side of the house toward the barn. "We've got to get to them before that sun goes down.

"Jon, why don't you and Elias get the woodshed, then come and join me here."

After allowing the sun to warm her face and rejuvenate her spirit, Mahal returned to the kitchen to prepare for the later meal while the men labored in the deep snow through the long afternoon, digging out access to the barn where the horses, two milk cows, chickens, pigs, and Hans' beloved cats had sheltered. Though the horses and livestock had been days with little food and water, they looked to be in good shape.

Hans wasted no time lighting a fire in a large galvanized tub, and when enough snow had melted, he filled troughs with the fresh water and let the animals drink their fill. By now, the woodshed had been dug out enough to get to an opening where they could pull out the logs, and Mahal had rejoined the group, gathering up buckets of oats while Jon and Elias threw bales of hay down from the loft and mucked out the stalls. Mahal threw a bridle over Wind's muzzle and walked him around the barn, talking in low reassuring tones like a mother to a child.

"Hans," Jon shouted as he rolled a bale of hay into the first, clean stall. "Throw me your knife, I need to cut this baling twine."

"Don't have it," Hans answered, glancing up at Mahal who froze in her tracks and turned her face toward him when she heard the exchange. "Dropped it in the snow on my way home."

Jon was about to comment, knowing how much the knife meant to Hans, but he caught the same silent exchange between Hans and Mahal that he'd picked up earlier and filed it away in his head with his growing suspicion.

"Here Jon, take mine," Elias pitched a large jack knife down from the hayloft.

Hans breathed a huge sigh of relief when his story went unchallenged.

With the barn and woodshed tended to, the men set out to shovel a path from the barn to the kitchen door, but the snow was hard and deep, and it was slow going. Hans returned to the barn for better shovel.

He was only a minute out of earshot when Jon stuck his shovel in the bank and wiped his forehead with the sleeve of his coat. "Elias," he said, "Have you noticed anything different about Mahal?"

"I don't know. Not particularly." Elias paused and took a minute to think. "Like what?"

"I'm not sure. It's hard to say exactly, but she strikes me as different, like something's changed. I don't know. Before the storm, she had seemed to be coming out of her shell, and now I can't even get her to look at me."

"You know her better than I do, Jon." Elias shrugged. "I never could get much of a read on her, but you'd be acting a little strange yourself if you'd been stuck out here through that blizzard. Hell," he laughed out loud, "you'd be downright loopy if you'd been stuck inside with Hans for three days. Tight-lipped as he is and shy as she is, I'd be surprised there was a word spoke between 'em."

"I guess you're right," Jon sighed, picking up his shovel and tossing a load of snow over his shoulder. "She's probably just kind of shell-shocked."

"Wait 'til things are thawed out," Elias went on. "This is the first day anyone's even been able to open their door without a fifty mile an hour wind blasting in their faces. She'll come around."

And then Elias paused. "Probably anxious to see that husband of hers. Lord knows it'll be awhile before she can do that, I'm sure. Unless we have a big thaw anytime soon, no tellin' how long it'll take to get the roads open."

"What do you say we hang it up," said Jon when Hans returned with the shovel. A shiver of cold coursed through his body. "I sure am feeling the chill now."

"Yeah," Elis agreed. "Time to call it a day. Snow ain't going anywhere soon."

The sun was just beginning to set beyond the largest drifts and the temperature had already dropped by several degrees.

After storing their shovels in the barn and feeding and watering the animals one last time, they trudged back to the house, where Mahal had set the kitchen table and laid out two pot pies she'd baked along with the roasted rabbit. The men drew up their chairs, hungry and tired after their hard work, and Jon looked forward to another opportunity to connect with Mahal. He used to love to sit and listen to the minor details of her day, precious moments that fed his fantasy of a future with her. The hearty meal did nothing to warm her demeanor though, and Jon resigned himself to calling it an early night.

CHAPTER EIGHTEEN

After dinner, the men offered to help with the dishes, but Mahal shook her head and scrubbed up the kitchen herself, then retired to her room early, anxious to avoid any more of Jon's attention. All she wanted to do was be alone with her thoughts. Exhausted, she lay on her bed and tried to will herself to sleep, but when she closed her eyes memories of the last three days kept her wide awake. She felt that she had made such a mess of things, and the more she pondered the details of all that had come about since her arrival at Gustafson Corridor, the more she wished she would never have to get up and face another day. Life on the reservation had been so much simpler. But her husband had grown into a different man than the one she thought she had married, and now she dreaded going back to him. She wanted Hans more than anything.

I love him so, she thought. *As much as any woman could love a man, and I know he loves me, too.* But how could she stay here? The brothers could never be reconciled after what had happened. Jon's heart would be broken, and she worried that Hans would grow to resent her for the role she played in the loss of his brother who had always been such a huge part of his life. She hadn't intended anything like this to happen, and yet it had. The weight of it all bore down on her as she finally drifted into sleep with one tired, lingering thought playing over and over in her mind: *What am I to do now?*

Worn out from the previous day's events, when Jon rolled over and looked at his pocket watch the next morning, it was already eight o'clock. By the time he got himself into the kitchen Hans was up and dressed pouring himself a cup of coffee. Elias had already heated up the pot and was busy loading a small backpack with a canteen of water and a sandwich Mahal had wrapped up for him the night before. When Mahal heard the men rustling about, she dressed and descended the staircase just in time to see Elias tightening the rawhide lacings of his snowshoes to ready himself for the trek back to Duluth where he planned to catch the sled ride home to his wife and kids.

"I reckon the next time I lay eyes on you, it'll be spring," Elias said to her. "The baby's turned out to be a hearty girl. I bet you wouldn't recognize her anymore she's so big. I meant to say it before, but Martha always tells me that if I'm ever to run across ya, I'm to say 'hello.' She sure was grateful for your help."

"I appreciated the opportunity," Mahal replied, wrapping a shawl over her shoulders as Elias gathered up his things and stepped out the door. "Please tell her I said hello, too."

"Yes," said Jon. "Please give regards from all of us."

"Will do," he said. "And we can all pray for an early thaw!" Elias waved as he pushed himself forward, the teardrop-shaped snowshoes distributing his weight evenly across the snow. They would be worth their weight in gold over ravines and hills where the snow was deep and walking on anything other than snowshoes would be almost impossible.

Back inside the house Jon, Hans, and Mahal muddled around in a wall of tension, and Hans hurried for the door. "The going will be easier if you let the sun heat up the snow a bit. Why don't you wait an hour or so, and I'll go out with you?" Jon said to him.

But his brother brushed off the suggestion. "I know Jon, but I've been cooped up too long. Gotta' get my blood pumping. I'll tend to the barn chores, but then we've gotta' dig out the rest of the woodshed before nightfall. There's only so many hours of daylight, and it's wasting."

"Damn, he's bull-headed," Jon said out loud as Hans pulled the door shut behind him. He was annoyed at Hans' sudden exit from the scene and wished they'd had a few moments to connect and prioritize their tasks. "I guess the woodshed's the only thing we got to worry about right now!" And then, minutes later, when Mahal drifted upstairs to her room he grew even more agitated, although he couldn't pin point what it was that bothered him most. Every time he thought about the glances between Hans and Mahal he felt his jaw clench and an irrational fear threatened to take hold of his senses. He knew it was ridiculous to worry. He had never heard Hans utter more than ten words to Mahal, but those looks between them seemed to hide a story. He had no claim on Mahal, and so, he decided to set his thoughts aside and carry on as if nothing had changed. He hoped that in resuming their old routines a regular course of life would return.

As the week wore on, the stress in the house grew palpable. Hans was cordial, but standoffish and shoved himself out the door every chance he could under the pretense of having to "size up the damage of the storm" while Mahal hung back, growing more silent and indifferent every day, until she was paying little attention to either one of them.

Shut in with the men, Mahal could hardly bear the detachment between her and Hans. Nor could she stand the pain she knew she was causing Jon every time she shied away from his attempt to connect with her. The volumes of heavy snow and the still un-cleared roads made riding back to the reservation impossible, and she went about the business of the house in a fog, spending as much time as she could alone in her room, increasingly desperate to avoid those times when the paths of the three of them were most likely to cross.

Hans strapped on snowshoes and headed out every day, gone for hours at a time, sometimes only returning as supper was being placed on the table and speaking minimally about where he'd been or what he'd done. For the most part, order in the house had been restored. The window in the living room was repaired on the second day, and Hans, Jon, and Mahal had resumed sharing their meals in the dining room. After dinner, Jon and Hans once again lounged in the living room over their precious glasses of Scotch, sipping slowly, and brainstorming ideas about expansion and development of their holdings. Other than that the brothers talked only about what they had planned for the next season: Hans' planting some of the felled acreage for the first time and Jon's putting a garden in the field behind the barn. It almost seemed like old times, and Jon's suspicions about Hans and Mahal were reduced to a low simmer. There were times though, in the quiet of his study and in those dreaded wakeful hours after a disturbing dream, when he was haunted by the looks he had seen pass between Hans and Mahal right after the storm. No matter how hard he tried to dismiss the memories, they festered and became fodder for his despairing sense that there was something more.

CHAPTER NINETEEN

Three weeks after the blizzard had passed, they finally got a break. Splinters of light sliced through the forests like swords pitched to earth, and a golden arch of sun inched the temperature up into the low forties. The warmer weather lasted days and the temperature climbed higher still, forcing icicles to drip from springy branches and lifting household moods. Paths were etched in the countryside, and main roads were cleared enough to be serviceable by horse and horse-drawn jumper sleds. Hans, as moody as ever, took turns with the horses, riding them into the fields to hunt rabbits and prairie chickens to supplement the canned and smoked meat in the cellar. In the afternoon, he often saddled up Wind for Mahal to take for a short ride down the long driveway and onto the county road where the hard packed snow was finally beginning to melt.

By the end of the second week, Hans had come back from town with news that Drake had closing papers for them to sign on the mill land. They had not received any food supplies other than what Jon and Elias had brought with them on the sled and what Hans contributed from his hunting outings, so an extended shopping excursion was put on the agenda as well.

"Will you come with us?" Jon asked Mahal. "It would help a great deal if you did the shopping while we meet with Drake. I'd like to be back here before the sun sets, and it gets too cold to travel."

"I don't know," Mahal answered. "I'm not sure I'll buy the right things." It wasn't that Mahal didn't want to go. She was anxious to be out of the house, but the thought of purchasing food supplies on her own in a crowded, bustling city like Duluth was intimidating.

"It'll be easy," Jon insisted. "I'll write out a list for you. We have credit with the grocer and the butcher as well. All you have to do is tell them what you want. I'll get Finn to help you. When everything's packed up, he can carry it to the wagon for you. Besides, it will be good for you to get out after being cooped up in here for so long."

Hans was thrilled that Mahal was coming along. Sitting with her wedged in between himself and Jon ignited the fire inside him that he'd fought so hard to contain these past few weeks, and it was all he could do to restrain himself from reaching over and, at the very least, take her hand in his. Just before noon they pulled into town, the three of them hopping down to the slushy street below followed by Finn from out of the back.

"Buy anything you want," Hans whispered into Mahal's ear, tucking a rolled up twenty dollar bill into her hand while Jon gave Finn instructions. "We'll meet you at the Spaulding around four o'clock. Just wait for us in the lobby. Finn will tend to the horses and wagon and help you with the packages."

Mahal, grateful that she had Finn for help and support, quietly handed her list to the shopkeepers, waiting in the background as they sorted and packed the various items, taking their time to get it right, then lending Finn a hand with the smaller boxes and sacks. Mahal soothed the horses as the wagon was loaded, and she considered trying one of the several wrapped caramels the grocer had pushed across the counter toward her. She had dropped them into one of her coat pockets, careful to keep them separate from the money Hans had given her. It seemed as if everyone in Duluth was in a good mood, happy to finally welcome the warmer weather, and the streets felt alive and festive. After a couple of hours all of the supplies had been purchased, and the wagon held a full load.

"I'm going to drive the wagon over to the hotel," Finn told her. "There is a covered shelter there where I can water and rest the horses before we head back to the farm. Mr. Gustafson mentioned you had more shopping to do after this, so I'll just see you back at the hotel around four."

Mahal watched as Finn moved the wagon forward, a little bewildered about how to fill this hour of unscheduled time alone in the city. Her eyes widened when she reached into the pocket of her coat and realized how much money Hans had pressed on her. Discretionary dollars were as foreign to her as idle time. Every penny she'd ever held was earmarked for some utilitarian purpose: an item of food, a yard of fabric, or the medicine the white doctor had set aside for her mother-in-law. A twenty-dollar bill to spend on herself left her a little nervous. It was also unnerving since it was the first gesture Hans had made since Jon had come home that let her know he still held her in his heart. There had grown a chasm between the everyday life she had resumed and the love that ached inside of her. Knowing that Hans still cared left her head spinning.

The unforeseen money and free time boosted Mahal's spirits though, and she found herself surprisingly eager, after a time, to join the small groups of humanity that filtered through the streets. After three weeks of being sealed up in the farmhouse, Duluth had never felt better. It looked as if every man, woman and child had taken to curing their cabin fever there and every storefront bustled with customers creating an atmosphere more attuned to the day before Christmas than a regular weekday. Any thoughts of doubt she had had about Hans faded as she strolled down Superior Street, fingering the money in her pocket with a lightness in her step she could not remember experiencing before.

Taking her time to peer over the snow piled up to the drugstore window, Mahal marveled at a robust waitress handing off cups of coffee and slices of tall meringue pies to diners perched on stools running down the line of the counter. How she would have loved to have gone inside and tried a piece herself or tasted the malted milk drink Jon had talked about. But she shuddered at the notion of going inside and sitting alone amongst so many strangers. *Maybe Hans will take me someday*, she thought, allowing herself the luxury of relishing in the fantasy as she continued to window shop.

Meandering down the block her eye eventually caught a sleek modern dress in the window display of **BAUER & COMPANY**. Mr. Bauer had taken pains to shovel all of the snow away from his storefront, and three young ladies about Mahal's age had stopped to gaze. "Oh, look," one of them said. "A slip dress with the dropped waistline. It's what they're wearing in New York!"

Though the dress was only a curiosity to Mahal, she wondered what other things the store might hold, and after several minutes of hesitation she got up the nerve to turn the door handle and step inside. Two fashionably dressed older ladies were dithering over stockings and handbags splayed out by Mrs. Bauer on a glass counter top as she walked past. The women paused and gave Mahal a long once-over before turning back around to resume their business. Mahal had never been in a shop such as this before, and she continued by to the opposite side of the room that held an entire counter of sewing notions as well as fabric and ribbon. "See over there?" she heard one of the women speak in a loud whisper. "That's the Ojibwa woman who's living with the Gustafson brothers."

"She's living with them?" said her companion. "Why?"

Mortified, Mahal drifted nervously around a corner into an alcove that featured a variety of women's millinery. Though she could only make out bits and pieces of the conversation, she could see the women's reflections in the hat mirror as they gossiped and shot furtive glances her way.

"I heard she was hired under the auspices of being their cook, but who knows what really goes on. All I know is that she lives there full time . . . alone with two single men."

"Well, she looks too young to be much of a cook."

"I don't think it's cookin' that's on their minds. Irma Grubb who works for Ramsey Drake says it's not a good situation."

"What do you mean? I can name five women who'd like to get their hands on one of those bachelors, especially the good looking one. What's his name, Jon?"

"True, but she's Ojibwa, for one thing. It's even worse than that though. Word is she's married!"

"What?"

"Shhhhhh! Not so loud! Apparently, she's married to an Ojibwa man laid up on the reservation over in Fond du Lac. Irma says Ramsey's got his hands full 'cause one of the brother's is in love with her and nobody knows what's going to happen."

"Well, she is pretty . . . looks kind of exotic . . ."

"Pretty's one thing, Ojibwa and married's another. I'm sure old man Gustafson's rolling over in his grave as we speak!"

"Cook," "Jon," "married." Mahal had picked up enough of the conversation to get a sense of what they were saying. She felt her eyes fill with tears, and she turned and rushed out, letting the door slam behind her. The women had confirmed her worst fear—people were talking about her. Her reputation reflected upon her people, but it was the trouble she was now certain she was causing for the brothers that bothered her most. Mahal's heart pounded as she tucked her chin down and hurried back to the hotel where she dropped exhaustedly into one of the oversized lobby chairs.

Hans smiled as he approached her thirty minutes later, his face flushed from the brisk walk from Drake's office to the hotel. "I was hoping you'd be here early," he said. "Jon is checking on Finn and the wagon, so we finally have a moment alone." He pulled one of the smaller chairs next to hers and sat down noting the look of trepidation on her face. "It's been a tough few weeks for both of us," he said, leaning in toward her. "I'm sorry if it felt like I was ignoring you while we're figuring things out."

"After all that had happened between us . . . I don't know. It was like you had run away, as if there was hardly a trace of you," Mahal said. "Of course, I understand you didn't want to do or say anything that would upset Jon. I didn't either, but the emptiness has left me uncertain."

"There were so many times I tried to find a moment to spend with you, but Jon was always around or you were off in your room. It's been torture for both of us. My heart jumps every time I see you."

She lowered her eyes as if she might cry. "It's just all so confusing. I was in one of the dress shops, and I overheard two women whispering about me living at the farm with you and Jon. It was so horrible. I ran out as quickly as I could."

"I'm sorry Mahal, people can be cruel. Look, I know the stakes are higher for you, but I love you. I meant what I said to you before. If you give me the word we can change all of this."

"But I'm not free," she answered, sadly. "I don't know if I have the strength to see it through."

"Mahal, I love you! I want to spend my life with you." Hans answered. "We can face it together. You can be done with your husband's abuse if you say you want to be with me." And when she did not respond, he said, "You know, every night I sleep, I dream of you. There is no more pretending."

"I love you, too, but Hans . . ." Mahal began, but her heart quickened and she caught herself in midsentence when she and Hans noticed Jon conversing with the attendant at the front desk. Jon bowed his head slightly and gave them a wave.

"Will you just think about it?" Hans said in a hurried tone. "Just promise me that."

"Yes," she said, as Jon strode toward them, his boots sounding on the wide-planked floor of the hotel lobby.

"You're here early," said Jon, sliding a chair up to join them, the misgiving in his voice obvious. "This looks like a serious conversation. Have I missed anything?"

"Not at all," Hans answered, pulling his shoulders back and turning his attention to Jon. "Mahal was just saying how challenging it was for her to be shopping alone in the city. She's okay though."

Finn walked up then, and they stood up to go, leaving Jon suspicious once more that there was more to the story than the one Hans had just told.

The ride back seemed much longer and more arduous to Mahal who couldn't wait to get home to the privacy of her room—away from both of them. She felt torn up inside. Sleep did not come easy that night, and Mahal laid on her side contemplating her situation until the darkness mercifully enfolded her.

CHAPTER TWENTY

Later in the week there were reports of more open roads, and Mahal made immediate plans to ride out to Fond du Lac that coming weekend. She was anxious to get out of the house, and though the reservation held its own problems, she thought that perhaps on the ride back she could collect her thoughts and sort out her feelings. It was clear to her lately that Jon was going to even greater lengths to win her attention and affection. Affable and kind, all he wanted was to see her smile again. There was nothing he wouldn't do for her, gently probing her when it looked like her spirits were low.

"What is it Mahal?" he'd say. "Nothing a brisk ride won't cure. Let me bring Wind 'round. The fresh air will do you good." He always hoped that she would ask him to join her, even seek out his company when she needed something, but she never did. And his heart grew heavy with so much love that had nowhere to go.

Some evenings the haunting sounds of Hans' bone flute could be heard drifting through the farmhouse, but in the mornings he'd strike out early, returning only for a quick, silent supper before meeting Jon in his study to discuss the business of the day, then retiring to the parlor to pour a tumbler of Scotch.

"I'm taking the wagon back to Duluth sometime this week," he told Jon one night. "I've got a load of fence posts to pick up at the lumber yard. Is there anything else we need?"

"Not that I can think of," said Jon. "Oh, and Mahal told me this morning that she'll be riding back to Fond du Lac on Friday," he added. "The roads are clear, so I guess she shouldn't have any trouble."

Jon noticed a flicker of emotion in Hans' face that left him with an uneasy feeling that was by now, not only troublesome, but familiar. Before Jon could provide any details of her imminent departure, Hans topped off his drink and went off to his room.

The following morning he rose early, intent on catching a moment with Mahal before Jon appeared, but his brother was already with her in the kitchen.

Though annoyed, Hans wasted no time getting to his point. "Mahal, I understand from Jon that you're planning on riding to Fond du Lac. I'll ride with you to the trailhead at the entrance of the reservation," he said with determination in his voice. "You'll be safer that way."

"You don't have to do that," she answered, throwing an uncomfortable glance in Jon's direction. "Looks like we'll have a few more days of thaw. I'll be fine on my own."

"It's not out of my way. I got business in town this week, and Friday's as good a day as any to go."

The jolt of such a plan left Jon seething, furious that Hans was suddenly revealing concern for Mahal's safety, and compounding his suspicion that there was something between them they were hiding from him.

"No!" Jon said. He couldn't help himself from protesting, but in an instant he realized how obvious and silly his reaction must seem. He quickly changed his tone. "I mean, you don't have to do that, Hans. She'll be safe on the roads, I'm sure. I would ride with her if I thought there was an ounce of danger."

"Probably, but since I got business in town," Hans said firmly, "there's no reason to take any chances in what still could be an unpredictable season. I'll see her to the trailhead."

Jon knew that Hans had made up his mind, and that challenging him would do no good. Unable to come up with a reason as to why Hans should not ride with her, he acquiesced. "Well," he said, "since you're heading into Duluth anyway . . ." He regained his composure and slid his chair out from the table, frustrated that complications such as these always seemed to persist.

Mahal nodded in acknowledgment, conflicted in her feelings of the anticipated ride with Hans, and she turned her attention to cleaning up the breakfast dishes.

Hans grabbed an apple and struggled into his coat. "I got work to do. I'll see you later," he said as he pulled the kitchen door closed behind him.

"You know I would have ridden with you if I thought there was any danger at all," said Jon the minute Hans was gone. He picked his empty plate off the table and walked it to the sink.

"I know," Mahal answered, "but there's really no reason for anyone to go with me when I can make it on my own. It is just by chance that Hans is traveling that way."

"Of course, of course! I didn't mean to imply . . ." Jon reddened, embarrassed at his clumsy attempt to spend time with her. He took a seat again at the table as he watched her work.

Mahal turned to face him, the beams of the morning sun casting a shadow on the contours of her face. "I have wanted to thank you," she said quietly, her doleful look only dulling the brightness of her eyes that he would always love. "You've been good to me, and I will always be grateful for the kindness you have shown me."

"It's been my pleasure," he replied. "I've never met anyone like you, Mahal. You deserve to be happy. That's all I've ever wanted to do for you."

He leaned back on the hard kitchen chair and watched her finish up while he mulled over what her thanking him in this way now really meant. Surely she would be returning after her visit to the reservation, so this was not a formal parting. And yet it felt vaguely like a goodbye to him, and he was afraid to pursue the conversation, preferring to live with the unknowns and unanswered questions than to risk hearing the word "goodbye."

CHAPTER TWENTY-ONE

The following night not even a wind gust stirred the ghostly silence that ran through Gustafson Corridor. It was well after midnight when Mahal, Hans and Jon were startled awake by Fjord barking frantically and scratching at the great front door. Within moments they heard a man shouting as his horse whinnied and neighed, stamping down on the hard packed snow, snorting smoky gray clouds into the air. "Mahal, get out here!" he yelled. "I'm not leaving without you. Mahal! Mahal!"

Mahal felt her heart racing and bolted upright in bed, the anger in her husband's voice terrifyingly familiar. The brothers yanked on their buckskins and boots, grabbed their pistols, and stationed themselves in the front parlor. It was clear that the man outside their door was Mahal's husband, and that he was prepared to do battle. Under the wide light cast by the moon, he reared his massive stallion and fired a single shotgun blast into the air.

"Goddamn," said Hans as he rubbed out more of the frosted window with his fist and narrowed his eyes. "What the hell?"

"The guy's crazy. Keep an eye on him, I'll be right back," Jon answered. He raced to the study and yanked two shotguns off the gun rack and a sixteen-inch Saxon blade their father had brought with him from Norway.

"I see you peering out that window. Come out of there and face me like men. I almost died because of you," the Indian ranted in an ugly tone. "And now you have my wife! What else are you gonna' take? I outta kill you both."

"Drunk," Hans mumbled to himself, but loud enough so that Jon could hear. "Drunk or crazy as hell. Maybe both. Either way it looks like he's healed up."

Seconds later the Indian was pounding on the heavy oak door, jabbing the butt of his rifle into the hard-grained wood. "I want my wife, Goddamn it," he demanded, beating at the door. "Mahal, come out. I know you're in there!"

In a fit of rage, Hans threw open the door and grabbed the man by the throat before he even knew what hit. Hans twisted his head and choked him down to the ground. The Indian flipped around, and the two men struggled on the porch, exchanging blows and breaking through the railing before landing in the snow. In a split second the Indian reached for his knife, slicing the air with wild, dangerous swings as he lunged at Hans.

Jon tried to get a clear shot from the porch, but it was too dangerous, and he tossed Hans the Saxon blade still in its sheath. In a single motion Hans swept it off the ground and drew it out before they went knife-to-knife. They fought on, the Indian flying into the air fierce and crazy, finally nicking Hans in the leg and drawing blood. Hans, livid, went after him with an enraged sense of purpose, wrestling him down, blade to his throat, within inches of killing him when Jon stepped off the porch, aimed his rifle high and fired a shot over their heads into the night sky.

"Hans, let him go. There'll be no killin' here tonight," he said, lowering his gun to the Indian's heart.

"Let me kill him, brother."

"No. Not on this land. We'll take care of him, but not that way."

Hans' eyes moved beyond Jon to the center of the doorway where Mahal had appeared, wearing a beaded tunic cinched over her deerskin leggings and a travel blanket held across her shoulders. Her belongings had been stuffed into a rawhide bag slung across her back. "Leave him," she cried softly, her voice quivering, her face stained with tears, her long hair tied loosely with a leather thong.

"Mahal! Get back inside!" Jon turned to go to her, but she held up her hand and stopped him.

"You choose, Mahal," said Hans, as he froze his grip on the Indian's throat. His voice was steady and firm, and he eyed her straight on, choosing words he had contemplated for weeks but hadn't been able to find the courage to say. "If you want to stay, just say the word. I'll either kill him or put him on his horse and get him out of here. What do you want to do? Your choice."

"He is my husband," she said, though she could not meet him with her eyes. "I have made too much trouble here already."

Hans loosened his grip as her response registered and slowly he stood up and backed away. The Indian spat at Hans' feet as he rose up himself, grabbing Mahal's arm as she walked past him, her eyes averted and head down. Pulling away, Mahal turned and met her husband face-to-face. "I want to get Wind," she stammered, her voice betraying the weight of the moment.

"Hurry up then," The Indian said, turning to mount his horse.

Mahal ran to the barn and emerged bareback on Wind, galloping off behind her husband as she had many times before.

As they watched Mahal ride off, Hans glared at Jon as he marched past him into the house. Nothing more was said that night, and the silence between them festered into the following morning until Hans finally saddled up his horse and spent the day with his foreman in the fields, riding into the farmyard long after the sun had set. By the time he set foot in the kitchen, his mood was as black as the sky. He was intent on grabbing something quick to eat and avoiding his brother by retiring directly, but when Hans opened the door he found himself face-to-face with Jon.

"Don't you have anything to say?" Jon asked him.

"Like I told you that first night . . . there's always trouble when it comes to women and Indians," Hans answered dismissively as he turned to walk away.

"It's too late for that kind of talk, now," Jon fired back. "Don't try to pretend you don't care about her! You're the one who asked her to stay!" He moved a step closer to Hans to drive his point. "You've acted strange ever since the blizzard, and now, it's all beginning to make sense. Something must have happened. I saw those looks between you. You tried to hide them, but I saw. And, you wanted to kill her husband last night? Kill him, Hans? That's not the reaction of a man who has no feelings for a woman. Now are you gonna' tell me what happened, or do I just have to use my imagination?"

Furious, Hans whipped around and lunged forward getting close up into Jon's face. "You don't know anything," he seethed, grabbing Jon by the neck of his shirt, then catching himself and releasing his grip.

"You asked her to stay," said Jon as Hans stepped back. "If you love her, why can't you just admit it?"

"Back off." Hans turned in the doorway to face him again.

"Well, I love her," Jon shouted after him, "and I'm not afraid to admit it. I'll always love her."

PART THREE
NATHANIEL

CHAPTER TWENTY-TWO

Eligible women in town still speculated about the handsome bachelor farmers, even more now that word had gotten out that Mahal had left suddenly. The brothers stayed tight-lipped about what had transpired that night, only telling Elias. He had asked if Mahal's husband had regained his health and if Mahal had returned to the reservation in Fond du Lac. Any thoughts or feelings the brothers may have harbored about her were swept under the rug, and they coped by throwing their energies into growing the land as their Pa had envisioned.

The brothers dedicated every waking moment to their passion of acquiring and developing land. Hans stuck his bone flute up on a shelf and never played again. Jon stayed away from Spirit Mountain and even the logging camp, riddled as it was with memories of Mahal. When they did shuck their boots and sit down with a lowball of Dewar's, they spent the time swapping ideas about the land and crops, the latest farm equipment, hired help, or the weather, occasionally venturing onto horses, trucks, or their current stash of the coveted Scotch. They did not speak of the Ojibwa or the reservation or the months they had spent with Mahal. Hans and Jon had loved the same woman, that much had become clear, but any private thoughts they had over the years regarding matters of the heart remained unspoken, loath as they both were to risk permanent damage to the tenuous connection between them.

One clear spring day, three years after Mahal had left, Hans was out on the range when he spotted a band of Ojibwa moving through on their way to set up their maple syrup camps. When he saw them a rush of the old passion erupted from deep within and, throwing aside his usual reserve, Hans walked his horse slowly beside them, scanning the squaws, desperately searching for the aqua-colored eyes that still haunted him. Some of the children ran alongside his horse and waved their small hands, but the adults only stared back at him, their eyes blank as stones, shaking their heads and then shuffling on when he periodically called her name. Hans stuck with the group for a good mile, overcome by a renewed desperation to be with Mahal again. He had often found himself distracted by his fantasies of giving himself to her again and again as he had that fated weekend, and memories of Mahal consumed him at unexpected times, like when he'd be selling a horse or just riding through an open field on a spring day.

Even after two years, he was overcome by a longing for her and found himself riding to the reservation at Fond du Lac looking for her.

"Her name was Mahal," he said, going from tent to tent. "Her eyes were light-colored, like the water in the lake." No one admitted to knowing so much as her name, let alone her whereabouts. After awhile, angry looks from some of the tribesmen made him uncomfortable, and he knew that he had to let it go.

Jon, too, was haunted by his memory of Mahal, turning his head at every dark haired woman he saw, once even trailing a young woman through the streets of Duluth. "Mahal?" he said, tapping the woman's shoulder. The woman turned in surprise and his heart sank. "I'm sorry," he sadly replied, tipping his hat in apology. "I thought you were someone I once knew."

Neither brother ever found love again. Never even sought it out. Family members talked about the strangeness of it all and occasionally tried to introduce them to single women they came to know, but the brothers were not interested. It was easier to be devoted to the land, expanding and acquiring at a feverish pace until their modest farm in Gustafson Corridor was a gentleman's estate with no luxury spared. The old farmhouse had been expanded too, and the family crest now boasted from high upon a giant river rock fireplace in the great room under a log-beamed ceiling. A carriage house and apple orchard were situated out back next to the old garden, all neatly laid out with horses grazing on pastures beyond, set off by miles of meandering white fence. Their status was enviable, but there was a great hollow emptiness to it all. If their Pa's dying words ever crossed their minds again, they never spoke them aloud. It wasn't the way their lives had gone, and it wasn't their way to talk about such things.

CHAPTER TWENTY-THREE

Over the course of the next twenty years the road to Gustafson Corridor was much improved, and though it was still prone to muddy ruts in rainy weather, its rolling hills and cultivated fields reflected the brothers talents as farmers. Even with all of their money and the sophisticated display of the house and grounds, the Norwegian frugality they had inherited from their father had served them well. Other than imported Scotch, the brothers' only other notable extravagance was an impressive collection of horses that they road and bred. They were always on the lookout for a well-built stallion to sire or a graceful mare to birth the perfect foal. It was on one such search that Jon drove a horse trailer to Bemidji, a small town out near the Mississippi headwaters, where he heard there was an Indian powwow and statewide horse trading show. Hans, who was working a land deal near Kettle River, planned to meet Jon there the following day, and if they were lucky, they'd be adding another prize to their fold. By lunch time Jon had already won a bid on a much talked about hot-blooded stallion called "Raindance," and he was about to leave the building and call it a day when a stunning palomino mare was led into the ring.

"Dreamcatcher!" The auctioneer's voice boomed through the microphone. "Here we have a real beauty! Splendid, yellow and tan . . . shiny cream mane and a tail to match. What do you say we have a nice opening bid for this stunner?"

Jon wasn't looking for a mare, but when the palomino's name fired memories of Mahal, he stopped in his tracks. Turning his attention once again to the auction block, his eyes widened at the sight of a magnificent animal. The horse held her head high, demonstrating a spirit he'd not seen since he first watched Mahal ride Wind to their farm.

As the bidding ensued, Jon battled head-to-head with a wealthy rancher who'd driven straight through from Denver intent on returning with Dreamcatcher. From the moment he'd set eyes on her though, Jon knew he would pay whatever it took to make the mare his. Back and forth the two men fought to out-bid the other until the price ascended to a staggering six-thousand dollars, and the rancher, swearing under his breath, declined to counter. When the winning bid was shouted out to Jon, he quickly tipped his hat to the rancher and then to the auctioneer.

"Step around and claim your prize!" It was the highest price ever paid for a horse in the state of Minnesota, and the thrilled auctioneer kept the momentum going with his quick repartee. "Absolute royalty folks!" he thundered at the murmuring crowd, many of whom had stood up during the bidding war and were still gathered close to the ring as if it were a boxing match. "Horses this good don't come 'round often, that's for sure!"

Jon worked his way through the crowd back toward a table decorated with an Indian blanket and set up with a saucy female cashier poised to take his money. He signed the necessary papers and scribbled his name on a ledger check. "Anything special I should know about her?"

"Dunno sir, but you can ask the owner," the cowgirl replied distractedly as she snapped her chewing gum. She pointed a long red polished nail toward the ring. "He's standin' right over there, sir," she said, the bracelets on her tanned arm jiggling with the snap of her gum. "See 'im? The good-looking kid in the black Stetson."

"Yes, ma'am. Thanks."

Threading his way again, this time to the back of the ring, Jon held out his hand as he approached the young man whose face was shadowed by his broad hat. "Jon Gustafson," he said, introducing himself. "I just bought your horse."

"Yes, sir, congratulations, but the horse doesn't belong to me. Belongs to a man named Earl Mobley. I handle and train all his horses, this one included. Mr. Mobley will be more than pleased, but you got yourself a real prize. She's a beauty. Smart too. Never had a horse so easy to train." The young man, who Jon guessed to be nineteen or maybe twenty years old rose to his feet as he said this and seized Jon's hand with a hearty shake. "Name's Nathaniel Bartell. Pleasure to meet you."

When Jon lifted his eyes in response he was thrown off by the blue-green eyes staring back at him, the same eyes that Jon had only seen once before in his life. Mahal's face flashed before him as they moved out of the crowd to find a quieter place to talk near the entrance to one of the stables.

"She is a beautiful horse all right. Anything special I need to know about her?" Jon was anxious to learn all he could.

"Well, she's a damn good horse," Nathaniel gave him a warm smile. "Beautiful to look at and, as I say, darn near trained herself. She has a solid temperament and rides quiet under the saddle. 'Bout the only thing I've ever seen spook her was a snake. Something about them spooks her something fierce. Luckily, the snakes are usually spooked by horses first though."

"Don't think I've ever met a horse that takes to a snake," said Jon. "Sounds pretty normal to me."

"Well, a little more than normal, I'd say. Keep your coiled rope off the ground." Nathaniel half-chuckled, pushing back the brim of his hat.

As Jon faced the young man there in the light of a high noon sun, the kid began fingering an antler-horn knife that hung on a leather sheath from his belt. Catching himself, he pulled a large envelope from his shirt pocket. "Let me give you Dreamcatcher's papers here," he said.

The sight of Hans's knife sent a shudder down Jon's spine, and he struggled to keep his composure as he spoke, willing his voice to convey nothing of the flood of emotion coursing through his body and mind. "That's quite a piece you've got there."

"Oh, yeah, thanks. It belonged to my mother," said the kid, flashing a smile. "Always brings me luck."

Jon paused, unsure of how to proceed with the conversation. "Your mother," he began, with his eyes still set on the all-too-familiar knife. "Did she teach you how to train horses too?"

"Well, no," Nathaniel answered. "She died havin' me, but she was a horse lover and had a way with animals, I'm told. I like to think I got that from her." Nathaniel turned toward the adjoining stable where the palomino had been led. "If you want to walk over, I'll introduce you to Dreamcatcher."

"Sure," Jon answered, with a tremble in his voice he hoped was not noticeable. Hearing that Mahal had died so young, left him shaken. As much as he wanted to know more, he knew it would be imprudent to ask, so he turned his attention to the business at hand. "I had no intention of buying a second horse. I actually came here for the stallion."

"You mean Raindance?"

"Yes, but the palomino caught my fancy the minute she was lead into the ring. How long have you had her under your care?"

"Mr. Mobley bought her when she was barely a year old. He let me name her, and I trained her myself. I've been around horses and ridin' since I was old enough to walk, but I've never seen a horse like Dreamcatcher. She's something special. I'll be kinda sorry to see her go."

The shocking revelation of who Nathaniel was trumped anything Jon could ever have imagined, and he walked alongside the boy, their boots crunching down on the pebbles and straw, Jon's gut in a jumble of anger, betrayal, and deep sadness. He had struggled for so many years to come to terms with the loss of Mahal and the questions about her relationship with Hans, but now here was this boy with Mahal's eyes, carrying Hans' treasured knife. The truth of their relationship now undeniable, Jon was livid and wanted nothing more than to pick up the horse, pack her in the trailer alongside the stallion, call Hans and tell him to meet him at home, then confront him with all he now knew to be true. But he wanted all the facts, and so he decided to press for more.

"So your Pa raised you alone then? Taught you how to train a horse?"

"Nope. Never knew my real Pa either. I was raised right here by the Lutheran Minister, Pastor Edwin Bartell, and his wife, Coral. They adopted me and gave me my name and were the only parents I ever knew, God rest their souls. A stroke took Mama Coral's life when I was thirteen, and the Pastor died two years later. I'd been working on and off as a hired hand for Mr. Mobley, and when they passed he was kind enough to take me in and give me steady work training the horses. Dreamcatcher was the first one he let me name."

Jon could feel the wheels turning in his head. It all made sense, and the realization of what happened between Hans and Mahal filled him with rage. Jon had loved her, truly loved her, and it had taken everything he had to hold back, keeping his distance, trying to be respectful of her situation, always believing that his patience would pay off. Then, in the course of three days Hans had taken advantage of her. Jon was furious, and he stewed as he struggled to maintain his composure with Nathaniel.

CHAPTER TWENTY-FOUR

Jon and Nathaniel entered the stable, its rows of identical stalls lining both sides, the aroma of leather, hay and manure strong in the air. Jon breathed the familiar scent deep into his lungs, hoping to clear his mind. The palomino was in the second stall, looking even more a champion than she had at a distance, her coat glistening in the shadowy light of the stable. Nathaniel unlatched the wooden gate and stroked her neck. "Hey, girl," he said. "I got someone here I want you to meet."

Jon watched as Nathaniel scratched Dreamcatcher behind her ears, ran his hand down her back, then over her flanks and legs. The graceful horse nodded her head and gave Jon a good sizing up. To Jon, Dreamcatcher was every bit as sound and well balanced as he remembered when he first caught sight of her at a distance from the auction block.

"Why is Mr. Mobley selling her?"

"Well, he hated to, that's for sure," Nathaniel answered slipping a bridle around her head. "But he's getting on in years, and it's time for him to begin thinning the fold. He knew anyone who could recognize how unique she is and could afford to pay a good price would more than likely take good care of her."

"Well, you can tell him she'll be going home to a large spread and will have her own stall in a heated barn that it took us three years to build," Jon told him. "My brother and I've got four stable hands who do nothing but look after the horses that only we ride. She'll receive the best of care, I can promise him that."

"Well, Mr. Mobley will be thrilled with that news. Come on, let's take her out and see what she can do." Nathaniel cinched the saddle and led Dreamcatcher out of the stall toward the open door of the stable. "How are you going to ride her?"

"Mostly trails. I used to bow hunt up Spirit Mountain, but now when I go out I like to keep to the foothills and woods."

"She'll be perfect for that. She's athletic, a great mover, but she's not afraid of heights either, if you ever decide to take her up. I've ridden her high around the Buena Vista ridge many times."

"Oh yeah? Maybe we'll head that way tomorrow when my brother shows up."

Nathaniel walked the palomino out toward a path that wrapped around the building and roped into a large open pasture. When they got to the edge of the field, Jon hitched himself up into the saddle and nudged Dreamcatcher forward with his legs. They took off into the open field kicking up a squall of dirt in their wake.

After several rounds through the field, Jon trotted the palomino in and Nathaniel greeted them, holding Dreamcatcher's bridle as Jon dismounted. "She's powerful!" Jon was all smiles. "What a performer. I've never ridden a horse so smooth and fast."

"She'd be hard to beat," Nathaniel laughed. "She loves a good run. Do you mind if I take her out one last time?"

"Please do. I'd like to see how she moves from a distance anyway. I find I can tell almost as much about a horse from watching someone else ride as I can when I'm on her myself."

Nathaniel handed Jon the reins and moved around Dreamcatcher's side and began loosening the leather bindings on her saddle and sliding it to the ground.

"No saddle?" said Jon.

"I prefer to ride her bareback." Nathaniel laughed, as he jumped onto Dreamcatcher's back. "She's comfortable either way."

Jon watched them fly with the word "Ojibwa" ringing in his ears. *He rides just like her,* he thought. It was almost too much to take in, and yet here it was—the truth galloping straight toward him. Nathaniel was living proof that Mahal had made love with Hans during the storm, and that more than likely, she had loved him as well.

After a good long run, Nathaniel pulled Dreamcatcher to a stop in a puff of dust. "What'd I tell you," he said, with a smile. "Most athletic horse I've ever ridden."

"If your mother had lived, she'd think you were half Indian." Jon covered the weight of the comment in a light-hearted laugh and then waited to see Nathaniel's reaction.

"I actually have Indian blood in me," Nathaniel said, gazing across the back of the horse at Jon's face, which had suddenly gone pale. "My mother was half Ojibwa and she married a full-blooded

Ojibwa man. Story goes though, that when I came out lookin' like a white man's son, the Indian threatened to kill me. Would have killed my mother too if she wasn't already dead. The Indian's mother saved my life. Brought me to a church that very night 'fore he could get his hands on me."

Jon felt as if he'd been sucker-punched, but he managed to hide his true feelings as he'd done so effectively all his life. "I once knew an Indian woman," he started off slowly, cautiously, "half Ojibwa, half white. She had eyes same as yours and loved horses, too."

"You knew my mother?"

"I think I did." He raised his eyes to meet Nathaniel's. "She used to work for me and my brother."

"Are you sure? How do you know it was her?"

"Yes . . . uh, I believe I'm about as sure as you can get. She was married to an Ojibwa man at the time, but it was not a good situation," Jon went on cautiously, slowly, steeling his eyes on Nathaniel, suddenly imagining what it must be like for him to hear this kind of information for the first time. He turned away, pacing back a step. "I knew her."

Nathaniel's attention was now completely on Jon, and with an urgency in his voice he set to questioning him. "What can you tell me about her? Please, sir. I sure would appreciate hearing anything."

Jon paused, considering what he could share. "She was a beautiful woman," he finally choked out. "I can tell you more, if you'd like . . . but let's talk in the morning. I've really got to get going."

"Please, sir," Nathaniel was close to begging now and he knew it, but he felt desperate. "Let me buy you dinner tonight. I've never met anyone who knew my mother." Nathaniel persisted, anxious to hear whatever Jon had to say about her. "M & J Steakhouse, first left in town, about seven. Whad'ya say?"

"Thanks, Nathaniel, but I have other business to attend to this evening." In truth Jon had nothing else to do, but he needed time alone to collect his thoughts and figure out how he was going to handle this. "I got my brother coming in tomorrow morning. He's as much a horse lover as your mother was, and I know he'll be anxious to take the palomino out once he sees her. Maybe we can meet later in the day, say around four? Give us plenty 'a time to wrap up. We can talk some more then."

Nathaniel wanted to continue to press Jon, but was afraid to anger him and risk losing the chance to hear more.

"Sure," said Nathaniel. "I'll make sure the groom has the horses ready to ride. Your brother might have a few questions about Dreamcatcher too, so I'll be sure to come around the stable later on."

"See you then," Jon answered, in a hurry now to take his leave. "Four o'clock it is." As Jon walked away something else occurred to him. Turning once again to Nathaniel, he summoned his courage to ask the question he already knew the answer to. "Can I ask you something? When were your born?"

"December 18th, 1921. Why do you ask?"

Doing a quick calculation, Jon felt a nausea rise in his belly and once again he found himself struggling to control emotions that threatened to undo him right there in front of Nathaniel. "Just curious," said Jon. "See you tomorrow."

That night Jon tossed and turned as memories of Mahal consumed him. He remembered every detail of how her eyes had captured him at the camp store and how he'd fallen for her so completely on the ride back to Gustafson Corridor. His mind was flooded with memories of how he had grown to love her in the weeks and months that followed. It was the first time he'd really understood what his Pa had spoken about on his deathbed. One day he'd not had a clue what love was about, and then, out of the blue, Mahal had appeared and changed everything. He'd been hit hard, and his love for her had consumed his life all these years. Not a day had gone by that he hadn't thought of Mahal, and today, looking into Nathaniel's eyes, it was like he was getting a piece of her back again.

As nourishing as the memories were, however, they were imbedded now with memories of the looks that passed between her and Hans in the days after the blizzard. Alone in his hotel room, Jon imagined what had gone on between them those terrible days of the storm when he was stuck at the Spaulding Hotel with Elias. A rush of anger burned through his veins like a fever. Mahal should have been his. He had respected her enough to keep his distance all those months, and Hans—who'd shown nothing but contempt for her—made love to her without regard for anyone other than himself as soon as the chance presented itself. Hans couldn't have loved her the way he did. He just used her, got her pregnant, and abandoned her. Why hadn't he gone after her if he loved her so much? How could he have made love to her and then let her ride off with her husband? What kind of man was he?

By the time dawn broke, Jon had slept little. He was seething as he shaved and dressed, preparing for Hans to arrive, and when he heard the knock on his door at a quarter past nine, he still had not made up his mind how to approach him.

"Hey," Jon said coolly as he unlatched the door. Hans strolled past him and plopped into a corner chair near the window.

"You 'bout ready?" Hans lifted his cowboy hat and set it on the small table next to the chair. "I got a hunger hanging out bigger than the Paul Bunyan statue that greeted me on the way into town."

"Let's go," said Jon, unable to look his brother in the eye. He turned his back on Hans to collect his own things. "Why don't we drive to the north shore of Lake Bemidji? It's only a few miles and close to the auction site. The horses are still there in the holding stables. I hear Ruttger's Lodge serves a great breakfast, and it overlooks the lake."

"You got viewing the horses built into this day?"

"Yeah, but later. After we eat." The mere sight of Hans rubbed raw feelings that spurned curt answers, and Jon found it difficult to even be in the same room with his brother. "God, you're so impatient, Hans. One thing at time."

"What are you so testy about? I thought this was a productive trip."

"It was," Jon answered, picking up his hat and making for the door.

"What'd you end up with?"

"Two beauties."

"Two, huh? Well, I'm right behind ya. You can fill me in on the way up."

The brothers climbed into Hans' pickup truck and took the leisurely drive to the Ruttger's Birchmont Lodge, a picturesque fishing and boating resort that settled along the north shore of Lake Bemidji. Hans ordered the Paul Bunyan special: eggs, hash browns, and bacon with a short-stack of pancakes drizzled with the local maple syrup. Jon found himself too keyed up to eat and ordered only coffee.

"That's it?" Hans said to him when the waitress had left their table. "You're not eatin?"

"I'm not hungry," Jon answered, his head turned toward the large picture window that filled the front wall of the room. The lake was calm and clear, and through an open side window, they could hear the chatter of children playing in the sand on the narrow strip of beach outside. Jon waited until Hans had finished his last bite before he started in.

"Hans," he said, folding his napkin and looking up from his coffee cup. "I have something I need to talk to you about."

"What's that? I hope you didn't pay too much for those horses."

"No, that's not it. I . . ."

"Well go ahead little brother, spit it out. What is it?"

"I was wondering what ever happened to Pa's antler-horn knife. You know, the one he gave you as a boy."

"What are you talking about Jon? What's that got to do with anything here today?" Hans waved him off. "That was so long ago, I can't even remember what happened."

"No, but I think you do remember. You told me you lost it in the snow. That's what you told me and Elias when we were all in the barn after the blizzard."

"Well, if that's what I said, then that's what happened. But what does it have to do with buying horses at an auction?"

"I just wondered . . ." and then Jon lost his nerve and went quiet.

"It's a hell of a time to be wondering about something that happened twenty years ago, Jon. What's gotten into you since you've been up here? You're thinkin' about stuff that's long gone—makes no sense."

"I guess," Jon replied. As desperate as he was to confront Hans and force him to admit the truth about Mahal, it was so much easier to let it all go.

"Let's get 'outta here," said Hans, uncomfortable with this sudden line of questioning, motioned the waitress for the check. He tossed two dollars and his spare change on the table and stood up. "It's time to see those horses. I have a feeling I'm gonna' be pleased."

"We can take them out for a good ride, maybe head up to the ridge around Buena Vista. It's been awhile since I breathed the north woods high-up in the summer time. There are plenty of trails up there, too, and we can ride out straight from the stables. I got two good saddles in the trailer."

When the brothers arrived at the auction pavilion, they parked the truck and strolled over to the holding stables where they found one of the grooms brushing down Dreamcatcher. Her honey-gold coat glistened in the cloudless light of what appeared to be a promising day.

"Hello, Mr. Gustafson," said the groom, recognizing Jon from the day before. "Name's Tim. Nathaniel's over at the auction. Do you want me to go and fetch him?"

"Nice to meet you, Tim." Jon shook his hand. "Let Nathaniel tend to his business. We'll catch up with him later this afternoon."

"Well, he did mention that you'd be by for a ride." Tim ceased the brushing with a final hand pat to Dreamcatcher's rump. "She's about done here. I've got the stallion in the barn ready to go, too."

"Thank you," Jon answered, nodding toward Hans. "This here's my brother, Hans. He'll be riding Dreamcatcher."

Hans held out his hand for a shake. "Nice to meet you, Tim. I don't think I've ever seen a palomino, or any horse for that matter, as good looking as this one."

"Yes, sir," said Tim with a short laugh, giving Hans' hand a vigorous shake in return. "You and a lot of other people. She's had a steady stream of visitors since yesterday—like a movie star. It seems everyone wants to get a look at the most expensive horse around, and they all say the same thing, too."

"What's that?" Hans replied, adjusting his hat to shade his eyes from the sun.

"That she's worth every penny. Let me get her saddled up, and then I'll bring around the stallion. He's pure quality himself. They make quite a pair."

"You know the saddles are in the trailer, right Tim?"

"Yeah, but it's locked. I've been waiting for you to bring me the key."

Jon unhooked the trailer key from his keychain and passed it to Tim.

"Here, take the reins," Tim said to Hans. "I'll be right back. Nathaniel gave me orders to pack your horses with some supplies. If you're heading up to the ridge you never know what you might need. There's a canteen of water, good rope, a small ax, matches, a couple of apples. I hope you got a decent folding knife."

"Thanks," said Hans. He sidled up to the elegant animal and ran a hand down Dreamcatcher's back, then walked her in a small circle in order to get a good look at her. "Damn, Jon, she's gorgeous. Sounds like you paid a pretty penny, but if her mind's as keen as she looks, and she rides as good, she just may be the best horse we've ever owned."

When Tim returned with the saddle, he was followed by another groom leading the stallion, which was already saddled up and ready to go. The stallion's spirited side-step as they strode across the yard showed a feisty horse more suited to Hans' style of riding, but Jon knew he would want to put Dreamcatcher to the test, and so they mounted their horses—Hans on the palomino, Jon on the stallion. It was noon, and the sun was warm on their backs as they set out for an afternoon of riding.

The auction site was situated near a campground only about a mile from the base of Buena Vista, a wide, sloping bluff with veins of ski trails carved into the landscape. The brothers wound their way up along one of the outside tracks where the ground was elevated and timbered with pine. Ascending more than a thousand feet before a section of it leveled off, they walked their horses across a long, flat meadow, allowing them plenty of time to acclimate to the altitude. At the end of the meadow they picked up the trail again and pushed their horses eastward, skirting the backside of the ridge. The going was slow on the narrow flank of the ridge where off to their left the tall linear trees loomed, bending their long shadows over them as they rode, Hans trailing behind Jon. Jon periodically turned his head to take in the wide, tranquil vista that opened on their right, and in the silent beauty of such a space, his thoughts turned to back to Nathaniel. He realized that he still didn't know what he was going to do or how much he would share with Hans about all he had discovered. Memories of Mahal haunted him, too. Jon had been encouraged by her increasing ease around him before the storm hit. He was convinced that she was falling in love with him, but then, because of Hans everything had changed. Now, he knew why. The more he ruminated about those three days, the more furious he became. He realized that if he was going to say anything to Hans today, it had to be soon. They'd been out for hours, and the daylight would shortly begin to fade.

"I met someone yesterday," he suddenly blurted out.

"Who? A woman?"

"No. I met a young man, that I think you might want to meet."

"Who's that?"

"His name's Nathaniel Bartell. He's Dreamcatcher's trainer."

The trail was narrowing and both men instinctively slowed the horses to maneuver them through the treacherous pass. "When I met him . . . after I'd won the bid on the palomino, I noticed he had eyes the same color as Mahal's. Remember, Hans? I mean, who could forget eyes like that?" Jon paused and let the news sink in before continuing. "Interesting thing is he's part Ojibwa."

The significance of this information wasn't lost on Hans. His gut tightened and his mind struggled to grapple with this revelation as he tightened up on the reins a little more to maneuver Dreamcatcher into a more favorable position. Doing his best to feign ignorance Hans replied, "Interesting coincidence, but why the intrigue? What are you saying? That this kid is Mahal's son?"

"Maybe," Jon answered, his voice growing stronger as he jostled around on the high-strung stallion who kept stalling, not wanting to move forward on the narrow path. "But why don't you tell me?"

"What the hell are you talking about, Jon. How would I know?"

"Don't give me this crap, Hans," said Jon, the fury he'd been struggling to restrain now unleashing his attack. "He told me his mother died giving birth to him nearly nine months to the day of the blizzard. He told me she was half Ojibwa married to an Indian man, and that he was adopted and raised by the minister and his wife right here in Bemidji."

Hans' discomfort escalated as the undeniable truth unfolded. "I'll be damned, Jon, but so what! What does that have to do with me? Guess her crazy husband had his way with her as soon as he got her home. Probably one more attempt to claim her and keep her on the reservation for good. Come on, we've got to push around this bend before we can head back. The horses are spooked by the height."

"I don't think so Hans. There's more!" Jon was on a roll now, the fury in his voice startling the horses and causing the stallion to ignite a small avalanche of pebbles into the ravine below. "He said his father was a white man, and when he was born looking like a white man's son, his old man would've killed him, but for his ailing grandmother who brought him to a church before he could get his hands on him. When I met Nathaniel yesterday, he had Pa's antler-horn knife attached to his belt. Do you know what he told me?" Jon was yelling now, fury spewing from every pore of his body. "He said it was the only thing he had from his mother!"

Hans was speechless. The reality of what Jon was accusing him of hit him hard. He felt trapped in the truth of the accusation that was unfolding before him. Mahal had given birth to his son and died in the process. The horror of it made him nauseous and he felt desperate to get off the mountain and out of the wake of Jon's attack.

Jon ranted on, "I know we never talked much about what happened those days you were snowbound with Mahal, but I always wondered. I suspected something had gone on between you two, but I just couldn't believe my own brother would betray me like that, so I tried not to think about it. Goddamn you, Hans! You knew how much I loved her! How could you do it?"

Hans' face grew pale, and he held Dreamcatcher several paces back from the stallion who was again reluctant to move forward, stepping side-to-side and edging away from the sloping ravine. "Look, Jon, you don't understand."

"Actually, that's the problem. I finally understand everything!" Jon knew that the proximity of the ravine and the pitch of the argument was agitating the horses, but he couldn't stop himself. He hammered on relentlessly. "It makes sense, now, why you wanted her to stay that night her husband showed up."

"For God-sakes, Jon." Hans stammered in a last desperate attempt to deny the truth. "If the kid is anyone's, he must be yours. I don't know what you're talking about."

"Liar!" Jon lashed out as he half stood in the stirrups, whipping around as best he could to face Hans. "You damn liar! I can't be his father. I never slept with her!" Jon landed hard in the saddle, yanking back on the reins and causing the stallion to rear in a sudden, powerful move that disengaged the rope slung from the saddlebag. It dropped to the ground with a heavy *thwump*. At the sight of the rope coiled in front of her like a snake, Dreamcatcher side-stepped and then, trapped by the woods on one side and the ravine on the other, she reared, her front legs flailing dangerously.

"She's shying—" Hans yelled. "Jon, I can't hold her!"

As Jon turned his head, he witnessed the beautiful palomino rear her legs higher, then higher again, while Hans desperately struggled to gain control. Finally, in a desperate attempt to hang on he dropped the reins and wrapped his arms around Dreamcatcher's massive neck. The stallion was agitated, too, now, and it was all Jon could do to rein him in, rendering Jon powerless to do anything to try to help. As Dreamcatcher reared for the third time, Jon watched in horror as Hans lost hold of her neck and fell back, his weight throwing the panicked horse further off balance. When Dreamcatcher finally came down once again her front leg caught the edge of the trail, and she lost her footing completely.

Unable to hold on himself, Jon slid off the stallion and stumbled toward the ledge. "No!" he shrieked, as he watched both horse and rider first slide, then tumble over and over down into the long rocky ravine. "Hans, no!"

Horrified and frantic, Jon dropped to his knees and crawled on his belly as close as he could to the lip of ravine. "No," he cried, dust and tears streaking across his face. Jon trembled, his heart pounding in his chest as he lay there drowning in disbelief. "Hans," he moaned, gulping back sob after sob and cradling his face in his hands. "Oh, my God!"

Jon lay paralyzed. The air around him was quiet and still, disturbed only by his anguished cries echoing across the gaping canyon. When his sobs subsided but with terror still gripping his chest, Jon slowly backed away from the ravine's edge and stood up, brushing the rubble from his chest and legs. For a moment he felt as if his knees might buckle out from under him, but he forced himself to move forward as his eyes scanned the trail for the stallion that was long gone.

With no sign of his horse, Jon began the arduous journey down the mountain on foot. About a mile down, a stream of angry clouds blew in and hung low over the bluff. A streak of lightning cracked off to the west and dusk was beginning to veil the sky. Off in the distance, Jon could see dots of light twisting along the highway, but it would be over two hours before he was able to stagger to the edge of the road and hold his arms up to a passing car that screeched its brakes and took him in.

Twenty minutes later they rolled into the auction site where the lights of the stable windows blazed like lanterns in the darkness. The driver stopped short in the center of the yard and laid on the horn to draw attention, having heard the details of the tragedy from Jon. The sky was pitch black and several men came running over in response, including Nathaniel who had been there finishing business, long having given up on meeting with Jon and his brother. When Jon staggered out of the car, the trauma of the day was evident on his face, and Nathaniel rushed to meet him.

"My God, what happened?" said Nathaniel. A smattering of raindrops broke free from the ominous sky causing them all to hurry to take cover in the protection of the stable.

Jon looked up at Nathaniel, the pain of his ordeal filling his eyes. "My brother's been killed on the bluff," he stammered, his tears again flowing freely. "Dreamcatcher spooked and reared when the saddle rope fell on the ground. We were too close to the lip of the ridge." He wiped his face with a short towel that had been handed off to him. "We were arguing . . . Dreamcatcher shied up . . . lost her balance. It was slippery up there. Hans had a good hold of her neck, but the third time she reared she lost her footing on the ledge. She went over taking him with her. God, it was horrible."

The stable hands who'd gathered by then murmured amongst themselves as the details of what happened unfolded. "I'll call the sheriff," one man replied. "That's hundreds of feet you're talking about."

"I know," said Jon. "There's no way anyone could have survived a fall like that. Stallion's running loose, too." He briefly let his eyes meet Nathaniel's. "I don't know . . . it was horrific."

Nathaniel picked up his cowboy hat that had dropped from his hand to the floor and slapped it against his thigh to get rid of the dust and straw. "Your brother being such an experienced rider and Dreamcatcher such a fine horse," he said, shaking his head, "makes it hard to understand how an accident like this could happen. Jon, I'm so sorry. I hardly even know what to say. Don't worry about the stallion though. I'll round him up tomorrow. He's scared off, but he's up there somewhere."

In time, Jon let Nathaniel drive him back to the hotel. Grief stricken and tortured, Jon stared out of the window, his attention to focusing on the slap of the wipers and the pounding of the rain on the roof, grateful that Nathaniel respected his need for silence.

That night in his hotel room Jon left his torn, dirty clothes in a heap and soaked in a hot bath, struggling to release at least a modicum of the trauma of the day. Afterwards, he sat on the edge of the bed with his head in his hands listening to the rain spitting against the windowpane. Somewhere outside a coyote howled in the dark, an echo to his own inner turmoil. "Hans," he murmured to himself. "I'm sorry. I'm so sorry." A cold chicken sandwich Nathaniel had handed him sat on the end table untouched. He knew he needed to sleep, but every time he laid his head on the pillow, the vision of Hans and the palomino falling over the edge of the ravine played over and over, like a movie he couldn't shut off. The haunting images were so disturbing, that he just lay on his side until exhaustion blessedly overcame him, and he fell out dreaming of nothing at all.

Jon was still lying listlessly on his bed the following morning when he heard a knock on the door.

"It's us, Jon. Open up."

The familiar sound of Bjorn's voice filled his heart, and he jumped up and pulled open the door. As his brothers gathered around and hugged him, Jon felt the deep connection between them and knew that it was the only thing that had the capacity to heal him.

They broke down in the safety of each other's presence, and when they'd regained their composure, Jon returned to the edge of the bed while Bjorn and Emil pulled up chairs. Jon found it difficult to reiterate the details of the accident, but he plowed on as best he could, stopping at times to collect himself.

"The Sheriff came by about an hour ago," Jon told them at the end. "He took a team and a couple of mules out early this morning. They traversed in from a lower point on the bluff. The body's over at the funeral home here in town. We can let them know what we want to do."

"Well, I guess we need to call Northland in Duluth to make arrangements," said Bjorn. "They can bring him home, and we can bury him beside Ma and Pa. I'm sure that's what he'd want. When you're ready, I say we walk over to where they're holding his body. I can make the call from there."

CHAPTER TWENTY-FIVE

On their way out of town the next morning, Jon asked his brothers to stop by the stable knowing he'd find Nathaniel there. There were so many things that needed to be said, and Jon hardly knew where to begin. It was Nathaniel who broke through the uncomfortable silence first.

"I'm so sorry about the death of your brother. I didn't know him, but I'm sure he was a good man, you two being so close and all."

"I appreciate that. Yes, he was a first-rate man, and he made a great partner. I guess we were about as close . . ." Jon's voice trailed off as he struggled to hold back the tears that threatened to destroy his fragile composure.

Nathaniel respected the moment, then shifted the talk back to the more mundane. "You heading out?" he asked.

"I guess so, yeah. My brothers are waiting on me, but I wanted to come by and thank you for your help."

"No problem," Nathaniel said. "Where do you live?"

"We're about five miles south of Duluth," Jon replied. After a few ill-at-ease moments, Jon garnered the courage to say what he had come to say. "Listen, I know there are a lot of things you want to know about your mother, but I need some time. It's been a hell of an ordeal here these past few days. I know I promised you I'd tell you more about her, but now's just not the time. I'm sorry."

"I understand," Nathaniel answered. "I was just hoping that we could stay in touch and that maybe sometime down the road . . ."

"Of course, of course," said Jon, interrupting him. "I want to keep in touch, and I want to see you again. It's just that I'm kind of worthless right now. But I've got your number, and I'll give you a call before too long."

"I don't know what it is, Mr. Gustafson," Nathaniel said, "but I almost feel like I know you already, like you've been a friend for a long time."

"I feel that too," said Jon. "Bjorn told me you recovered the stallion, and I appreciate that. How's he doing? Is he in any shape to travel?"

"There's no doubt he was traumatized, but he'll be okay. Not sure I'd move him so fast though."

"I know," said Jon. "Those were my thoughts exactly. I was wondering if I could leave him here with you until things settle down. I'll pay for room and board. That's not a problem."

"It's done," said Nathaniel. "I'm sure Mr. Mobley won't mind at all. In fact, I'll get Tim to drive him over there this afternoon. Mr. Mobley's got a nice spread close by, up toward Red Lake. It will be good for the horse to be back in a peaceful place after what's happened."

"Thank you, son," Jon said. "I'll be in touch."

CHAPTER TWENTY-SIX

Jon spent the early days after the accident half-heartedly dealing with the more pressing business matters that he couldn't ignore. As the weeks wore on, it became evident that he didn't have the luxury of mourning the loss of his brother by indulging the depression that threatened to consume him. He had Hans' side of the business to deal with as well now, and the demands of both weighed heavily on his mind, forcing him back into his work, a familiar mode that brought him some degree of comfort. Running the business by himself was all-consuming, and there were many nights when Jon sat up burning the midnight oil, rolling the ice in his Scotch, eventually coming to the conclusion that the job was too big for one man. Even as he pondered the newly formed problems, a real solution eluded him. His brothers tried to help, but they didn't really know the business. And their lives were already consumed with their own endeavors and the needs of their growing families. Jon did not want to bring a stranger into the mix.

Months passed, and Jon continued to throw himself into the challenge of managing all of their holdings by himself. He tried not to think about the accident and all that had precipitated it, but when he sat down to eat a simple supper by himself each night, the solitude opened flood gates of memories of the accident and of Mahal and the son she had born.

Then, one morning he woke knowing it was time to come to terms with the unfinished business of his life. He picked up the phone and gave Nathaniel a call.

"Hey, Nathaniel," said Jon. "You've probably thought I'd forgotten about my promise to you, but I've been doing a lot of thinking."

Nathaniel's relief at hearing Jon's voice was evident in his upbeat tone. "Would you believe me if I told you that I was just about to call you myself?" he said. "I got a job offer in Montana, and

I'm planning on heading out there in a month. I wanted to get this stallion to you before I go. If you want, I can trailer-up and be in Duluth 'fore week's end. Tomorrow even, if that would work. I know you've had lots to deal with though, so if it's not a good time for you, I'll figure something else out. It sure would be good to see you, sir," he added.

"I appreciate your offer, Nathaniel. Of course, I want my horse, but I'd also like to get to know you a little better. Please don't take that job until we talk. I might have a better offer for you. What do you say I meet you in Bemidji tomorrow morning? I'll get up there early with a trailer and a good saddle horse. We can load up the stallion and drive to Big Sandy, catch a view of the lake, then ride on into Fond du Lac and Gustafson Corridor from there. We can take in some scenery and get to know each other a bit. If you can get Tim to drive the truck and the trailer home for me from Big Sandy I'll pick up the bill."

"That sounds fine to me," Nathaniel readily agreed. "I'd like to see Gustafson Corridor, and with that plan we can be out the better part of the day."

"Great," said Jon. "I'll meet you at the Mobley spread around eight, and we can take it from there."

CHAPTER TWENTY-SEVEN

When Jon arrived the following morning, Nathaniel led the stallion into the trailer and latched the door. Jon's heart sank at the sight of the magnificent animal who, through no fault of his own had played such a large part in altering so many lives. He filled his lungs with a long breath of the green morning air. It had been three months since he'd seen Nathaniel, and one of the first things he noticed was the antler-horn knife attached to his belt. At first, he thought it was the knife that reminded him of his brother, but then he realized that there were other things too, mostly the way Nathaniel carried himself, his husky build and the odd way he bit his lower lip when he contemplated a problem—so much like Hans it was unnerving and comforting at the same time.

They drove with the truck windows down, both a little nervous, each wondering what the other would have to say. The sounds of the road drowned out any chance of conversation, but a little Gene Autry came through on the radio. Jon kept the wheel steady, glancing sideways at Nathaniel, now and then rehearsing in his mind what he planned to tell him. They wound their way through the Chippewa National Forest on into Grand Rapids, then cut south, pulling up to Big Sandy around noon.

They lunched on roast beef sandwiches Jon had ordered with his breakfast at the local cafe that morning and sat by the side of the lake enjoying the peace and the beauty of the sun playing off the water. The sandwich, though, tasted dry in Nathaniel's mouth, anxious as he was to ask the questions about his mother he'd carried with him all his life. Jon ate in silence, clearly lost in thought, and Nathaniel held his tongue.

When they had finished their lunch, they saddled up the stallion and locked the extra saddle in the trailer as Nathaniel had decided to ride bareback. They took their time walking the horses to the trailhead. The water on the lake was calm. The sky clear. As Jon mounted up, he mercifully broke the silence. "I know an old Indian trail not too far from here," he told Nathaniel. "It'll take us longer to get there, but we can break at Tannen's Camp and let the horses drink in the stream that runs through." He hesitated then, knowing that what he was about to say would more than likely change the trajectory of both of their lives. "I've decided I'm gonna' to tell you the whole story, Nathaniel. I'm gonna' tell you the truth . . . everything I know."

"Thank you, sir. I sure would appreciate that," said the kid, smiling as he took up the reins and hoisted himself onto his saddle-less horse.

Jon pulled the stallion up beside him, and they booted their horses forward toward the trail. "You know, I rode part of this trail with your mother one time," he said as he turned his head to give Nathaniel a smile.

"You did?"

"Uh-uh. She was helping out at a logging camp on our land over near Leech Lake, which is where I met her. When I saw those blue-green eyes, I knew she was something special."

Authors Note

The Bachelor Farmers is a work of fiction. The story, characters, certain events, their timing, and settings are loosely based on the history of Norwegian immigration to Duluth, Minnesota, as well as the logging industry and the conditions that existed in that era. I've taken a writer's liberty to play with elements, real and imagined, to better suit the narrative. For example, Tannen's Camp is not a real place, though Spirit Mountain and other locations are. The 1918 Flu Epidemic was real, but the March blizzard at that time was not. I've allowed the Gustafson's to have run their own power line, though most farms in rural Minnesota did not have electricity in the early 1900s.

I began this novel as a simple love story surrounding two Norwegian brothers set in Northern Minnesota. When I delved into the history of the area at the time and saw the rich blending of the immigrant and native cultures against the beauty of the surrounding landscape, they quickly became an integral part of the story and the perfect backdrop for events to unfold.

Questions For Discussion

1. Hans and Jon never married, nor did they seem to have any desire to do so until Mahal came along. What was it in their upbringing that might have contributed to their bachelor status? What was it about Mahal that she was able to ignite such a powerful challenge to this status in both men?

2. Hans stepped in and became a father figure for Jon during the years they were separated from the rest of their family. Do you think this dynamic played a role in the ways things unfolded with Mahal?

3. Hans and Jon were profoundly affected by the presence of Mahal in their home. How did each of them change, both positively and negatively, as a result of having her in their lives?

4. Mahal's husband is abusive and yet she chooses to go back to him when forced to make a choice. What do you understand about the dynamics of abusive relationships that would shed light on why she may have made this choice? Is there anything Hans or Jon could have said or done that could have changed her decision?

5. Like the sisters-in-law, Jorunn and Marga, we all struggle with the issue of judgment: judging others and feeling judged by others unfairly. Talk about your understanding, from your own experience, of what motivates us to pass judgment on others, and what you have learned about the seductions and pitfalls of judgment.

6. What does it say about Hans and Jon that they were able to get past all that had happened with Mahal and still be business partners and live under the same roof? Do you know any women or men who would be able to do this? What would it take for you to be able to make such a choice?

7.   How do you think the accident changes the relationship Jon will have going forward with Bjorn and Emil and the rest of the family? Do you think the family will accept Nathaniel?

8.   What kind of relationship do you think Jon will have with Nathaniel? What do you think the future holds for them?

9.   What does all of this mean for Nathaniel? Do you think the discovery of his existence by Jon is a good thing for him in his life? What will be some of Nathaniel's issues as a result of learning the truth about his life? Is it always good to know the truth or do you believe that sometimes, some things are better left unrevealed? Do you know of any stories or situations where it was or might be better if the truth were not known? Was Jon's revelation to Nathaniel motivated by guilt, selfishness, compassion, or something else entirely?

10.   Describe Gustafson Corridor ten years after the story? Where do things go from here?

I would love to hear from you about your thoughts, feelings and questions regarding this novel. Please feel free to contact me at: brendasorrels@aol.com or visit my website at www.brendasorrels.com

Copies and E-reader versions of the book may be ordered through Lulu.com or Amazon.com.

The Way Back 'Round

Coming soon from Brenda Sorrels

The Way Back 'Round is a story of family and friendship, of a boy who makes an innocent, but terrible choice that haunts him for the rest of his life.

Set in rural Minnesota in the 1930s **The Way Back 'Round** follows the life of young **Jake Frye**, who enjoys nothing more than sitting between his father's legs, driving a wagon team of horses. However, when a large buck juts across their path and pitches Jake from the seat, his mother, tender from a string of miscarriages, reins him in. Jakes frustration builds and he makes a devastating mistake.

Rejected by his mother and wracked with guilt, Jake hops a freight train joining the thousands of men and boys riding the rails during this depression-era time. He meets **Franz**, another runaway and they become brothers. Picking fruit in California, cotton in Texas, they beg at back doors, eat in soup kitchens, sleep in "jungle" camps - all under the threat of brutal railroad "Bulls" who patrol the tracks. While Franz dreams about marrying a red-headed girl, Jake yearns for his family. When a kind farmer tells them about Roosevelt's Conservation Corps Camps set up to help young men like themselves, they head to California and join up.

Working in the camp north of LA, the boys have structure, shelter and steady food. They spend their free time at "Arnies", a beach bar in Santa Monica that caters to the camp boys and servicemen. Over French Dips and cold beer they meet soft-hearted **Bonnie** and brassy **Linae**, for whom Franz falls hard. As WWII escalates, the boys join the army where Jake's new life unravels and he again, must confront his past. **The Way Back 'Round** is told with great sensitivity and reinforces the truth that our lives are shaped by the choices we make.

About the Author

Brenda Sorrels grew up in Fargo, N.D. and attended Manhattanville College in Purchase, N.Y. She now lives in Dallas with her family, including small dog, Charlotte—and spends summers writing in Connecticut.